Bone Lake

Brad Walseth

Geryon Publishing

BRAD WALSETH

ISBN-13: 978-0-9986904-0-7
ISBN-10 0998690406

Special thanks to Melody for her love, patience and keen eye as an editor. Also thanks to Marcia, Harold and Debra Bernhardt and the Iron County's Museum's *Men, Mines and Memories;* and Al and Ruth Pieper and the Harbor House Museum for their great assistance with research into iron mining history and the tragic events that occurred at Mansfield. This is a work of fiction. Names, characters, businesses, events and incidents are either the products of the author's imagination or used in a fictitious manner. Although inspired by historical events, any resemblance to actual persons, living or dead is purely coincidental. Please also be assured that no animals were harmed in the writing of this work of fiction.

For "Flipper,"
wherever he may be…

CHAPTER ONE

*This is an evil among all things that are done under
the sun, that there is one event unto all: yea, also
the heart of the sons of men is full of evil, and
madness is in their heart while they live, and after
that they go to the dead. — Ecclesiastes 9:3*

The group of children laughed and jostled each other in the
sunshine as the boy watched them intently through the scope of his
rifle.

Sighing, Tim pulled back from his bedroom window and
placed the gun carefully back in the corner of the room before
flopping back onto his bean bag chair to engage another wave of
the mutants who advanced toward him in ever increasing numbers
on the screen on his computer. On the television, a skeletal figure
wearing the face of one of his victims dug his claws cruelly into
the torso of a screaming actress, projecting an amusing cinematic
fountain of blood into the air, but the young man just yawned.
He'd seen this movie too many times and had lost the thrill the
popular movie killers' brutal actions once gave him. Ignoring the
television, the boy's fingers flew frantically and his guns blazed
with extreme precision, as his muscular avatar cut down the
vaguely humanoid figures stretching their fingers toward him.
Cascades of blood, guts and brain matter spattered the walls and
covered the floors with puddles of gore, through which his avatar
strode onward relentlessly. Tim yawned. This level had once
offered a challenge to him, but now it was usually just something

1

to kill time until his bitch of a mother forced him to turn it all off and do his chores and homework.

After a few more minutes of mayhem, he hit the pause button, stood up and, hearing the voices outside, again approached the window. Raising the gun back up to sill level, he parted the curtains and checked out the kids gathered on the street corner again through the scope. He knew them all, classmates, friends of a sort, he guessed. He saw one of them was Albert—the tall one with the pimply face. He didn't really like Albert very much; the ugly-bully was on the 8th grade basketball team and sometimes teased Tim for being short. The curtains stirred as he moved the gun barrel further out the open window to where he put the tall boy's cratered face squarely in his sights. Below, the gangly youth laughed loudly; the boy watched as Albert's braces shone in the sunlight.

There was a younger boy with Albert; the boy recognized him as a student in his grade at school. Tom was a good guy; he and the boy liked some of the same video games and they had just exchanged some trading cards earlier that week at lunch. Tim wondered what Tom's mother and father were like, and if they would be sad, as he centered the crosshairs on the boy's grinning face.

The boys were engaged in teasing a pair of blonde girls; he knew them from school as sisters. Sally, the older one was real mean; he remembered how she had whipped him with a jump rope when he had made some dumb joke. He hated Sally. He squinted and made a bullseye out of one of the black ribbons she had in her hair and pretended to fire.

The younger girl giggled loudly, and Tim, hidden behind the curtains, turned his attention to her. Sally's younger sister, Sarah, was in 6th grade, a grade below him. The boy really liked Sarah and she seemed to like him too. She was always real nice to him and had very pretty blue eyes and a smile that made him feel funny inside. He aimed the gun at her and watched for a minute before lowering the weapon. He put the gun back in the corner safely like his father had taught him, before the bastard had moved away to Minnesota with his new wife. The boy thought of the man for a moment and rage filled his heart, before he regained his calm and retreated back to the world he felt at home in, the pixilated, monster-filled game that provided a welcome home and outlet for his anger.

On the television, a man using a rusty hacksaw cut off his own leg in a vain attempt to escape the villain, who appeared from the shadows to smash the man's head into pulp with a sledgehammer. The boy knew how the man felt. There just was no getting out of here, no escaping from the combination of rage and boredom that defined his existence.

His stomach growled, so he stood to go to the kitchen, but hearing the laughter from outside, took another glance at his four classmates standing in a circle on the sidewalk. Raising the rifle, he took aim and fired one quick shot. The burst exploded into the back of Sarah's head, ceasing the girl's laughter forever.

Oblivious to the panicked screaming coming from the street, the boy went into the kitchen and made a bologna sandwich, took a banana and a handful of candy off the counter and put it all in his lunch bag. As a siren sounded in the distance, he patiently put on his boots, camouflage hat, jacket and backpack, and carrying his rifle and a box of ammunition; he walked in numb silence out the back screen door, past the rusted swing set, the wading pool and the lifeless bodies of his mother and little sister and into the darkness of the woods behind his yard.

CHAPTER TWO

Jeremy Hawkins walked down the highway in the rain sticking out his thumb and growled as another car passed him, thinking to himself, *Fuck. Here I am. Going back to fucking Crystal Falls. And what the fuck for?*

He couldn't exactly blame anyone for not picking him up. It wasn't like he was Mr. GQ after all. His blonde hair still had a short and somewhat military type cut, but he was unshaven and dressed in cheap jeans, T-shirt and hunting boots that were a size too big—that was all he was able to obtain from a local charity after his release. A light windbreaker was plastered against his body and revealed the effects of several years of regular workouts in a gym. Yeah, he looked like a badass and had to admit that he wouldn't really want to pick up anyone who looked like him out in the middle of nowhere.

It wasn't terribly cold in the light rain, but the dampness was unpleasant in the wind, and the passing trucks and cars sent sprays of chilly moisture into the air. It felt strange to be out of uniform, and the mixture of giddiness at the rush of freedom and—he was surprised to discover— the fear of suddenly having no one watching over him and scheduling every detail of his life was disorienting. He watched warily for the Highway Patrol, who had already hassled him once on his journey, and wondered how far he had walked since the last ride had left him outside of Green Bay,

I told myself, that I'd never go back to this God-forsaken piece of Hell, he thought, *but then I didn't know then what I know now. And I have my reasons.*

4

A hot little sports car suddenly pulled over up ahead, and Jeremy had a momentary feeling that his luck had changed when an attractive young woman climbed out of the driver's seat. Taking a deep breath, he jogged painfully toward the vehicle on weary legs, his blistered feet aching. But when she got a good look at him, the woman's eyes widened with fear, she hurriedly threw a bundle into the tall grass, dove back into the car and drove away squealing her tires on the wet pavement.

Looked like a baby, he thought, startled, but when he bent to examine the bundle, it was just junk food wrappers and soda cans wrapped in plastic. *Story of my life*, he thought and continued walking slowly north as he pondered.

Like what got me sent up in the first place. My juvie record wasn't any too clean, but that little 'incident' surely was not entirely my fault. But then the pricks in charge around here, including my asshole step-father the Sheriff of Iron County of all things, wanted to try me as an adult. Good thing I had witnesses who didn't punk out on me. It's not like I was some huge, badass motherfucker either, but I am quick and I know where to hit 'em, gotta admit. Take after my old man that way, they say. Not that I remember the creep, who disappeared when I was just a toddler. Nobody ever figured out where the fucker went, but from the sounds of it, he finally ran into somebody he couldn't handle and went and got himself killed. But that's all a different story.

The young man trudged slowly onward. Cars passed him by, but he felt too tired to even raise his arm. He tried not to, but he thought about his father. People always used to tell him stories. It was always "Your daddy, Jesse Ray did this," or "remember that time Jesse done that," or "You look just like your daddy, Jeremy."

Actually Jeremy thought he got quite a bit of his looks from his mom, who only rarely ever mentioned his father's name, at least not without breaking into sobs. He knew he had grown taller than his dad. Based on stories he'd heard, Jeremy felt like maybe he was less impulsive and more careful in planning his moves, despite

5

his recent bad luck that got him sent up. But in any case, he had grown sick of hearing about his dad all the time from strangers, especially considering the infamous Jesse Ray's lunatic, out-of-control behavior had forced Jeremy to grow up without a real dad.

To make matters worse, he had to endure Roy Pultz, aka "Junior," his mother's 'husband.'

That lard ass hated me my entire life, he thought bitterly, *and made it very obvious—at least when Mom wasn't around or was passed out somewhere, that the sight of me made him sick, especially when some of my adventures embarrassed him in the public eye.* But Junior stuck it out because he had a thing for Jeremy's mom big time. She, on the other hand, only stuck around because the jerk kept a roof over our heads and always had what she especially needed to get through the ordeal of her life, as in plenty of drugs.

When Jeremy got himself sent downstate, he knew that it broke his mother's heart. Junior, however, was more than ready to see him sent up river for good, until it struck him that having a convicted murderer in the family, even just a stepson, isn't real beneficial when it comes re-election time. So he went all out campaigning for the "self-defense" theory and got Jeremy sent to a juvenile detention facility until he reached adulthood; and now Jeremy finally got "cut loose" a couple days ago.

I guess I can thank him for that, Jeremy thought, *but the last three years weren't exactly a picnic in the woods either.* Junior had made Jeremy promise he wouldn't come back after he was released, and the young man was pretty damn determined to keep his end of that bargain, but for one thing…

You see, Jeremy's mom, Jenny, had gone missing. *She just up and took off without so much as a goodbye to me or anything,* Jeremy contemplated. He knew that wasn't like her to do something like that, and as such, Jeremy's imagination ran wild with theories, among the worst being that Roy-boy, the harmless-looking, roly-poly clown—who in reality is the murderous drug kingpin who runs the town—must have done something stupid. Real stupid. Like hurt his mom. His heart tightened in his chest.

Jeremy knew that there isn't much that happens in Iron County without Sheriff Pultz's fat fingers right there deep in the middle of it. Junior had several members of the town on his payroll running drugs, and the rest with their heads so far up their asses that they were completely clueless as to what he was up to behind the scenes. A real piece of work that one. *Imagine growing up with him as your role model,* Jeremy thought to himself with a snarl.

Jeremy turned the facts over in his head again. He had called and got ahold of the fat fuck the other day because he hadn't heard anything from his Mom and was advised by the creep that she had taken off in her car a couple days ago, and that no one had seen anything of her since. His stepdad strongly advised him to stay away from town. He implied that he and Jeremy's mom had been feuding a bit lately, but that he was sure she would eventually turn up once she cooled off.

Junior also said he believed she was doing this to spite him, not that Jeremy would blame her, as he was currently embroiled in the tightest race for sheriff he had ever experienced. Some outsider—a former C.I.A. agent had recently moved into the area and was making waves about the problems—primarily drugs, rampant in Junior's fiefdom, and this uproar was causing some of the more decent town folks to start to think it might just be time for a change to be made.

Well, he should've known better, Jeremy thought and quickened his pace, *because him warning me to stay away was just about the stupidest thing he could've done.* He would get a ride sometime soon. And if he didn't, he would walk the whole damn way if he had to.

Jeremy marched ahead grimly into the face of the wind as the spray of rain grew harder.

I've grown up a lot over these last few years, and the freak doesn't scare me anymore. He's a fucking joke; a dangerous and ruthless one who has gallons of blood on his hands I admit, but a joke nonetheless. And if I find out he's hurt my mom... crusading CIA agents and wronged victims seeking revenge will be the least of his worries.

CHAPTER THREE

"Stay here, I promise you'll be safe inside," the man in the cap with the gray sideburns shouted in a hoarse voice as he pushed the frantic woman back into her seat.

"But sir," the woman protested as she brushed her hair out of her worried eyes and adjusted her long skirt to which a young boy and girl kneeling on the floor clung to.

"Listen to me. The train car is metal."

"But—"

"You are safest here. You cannot outrun it." He held up his hand as a chorus of feminine voices rose in protest. "No ladies, you must stay here and I will go and try to get help," the man spoke forcefully and with the full force of uniformed authority. Turning quickly, he tried to ignore the worried and tear-stained faces of the frightened women and crying children that filled the seats of the train car as he closed the door with a loud clang and locked it.

Jumping down from the step, the man ran down the tracks, watching over his shoulder as the bright glow approached rapidly, advancing toward the steam-engine train parked at the station, while inside mothers comforted their sons and daughters as best they could.

As the conductor reached the edge of the building, the brakeman appeared on horseback, struggling to control a panicked, wide-eyed horse that jumped and shimmied in terror.

"Let's go!" he yelled.

"Where are the engineer and station master?" the conductor asked.

"Gone already," the mounted man said and pointed toward the distance, where two men on horseback were riding away. "Climb up behind me. We must go now!"

The man in the cap shook his head as the towering wall of smoke and flames reached the edge of the meadow and hungrily devoured the prairie grass and bushes surrounding the railyard.

"The damned inferno is too fast, you can't outrun it, even on horseback!" the conductor said sadly with a shake of his head and removing his cap, he wiped the sweat from his eyes with it.

"I have to try," the brakeman said. "May God be with you then, Daniel!" he shouted over his shoulder and spurred his spooked horse to go galloping off toward the opposite horizon. "And with those poor souls in the car as well," he muttered to himself as he bolted furiously away with the relentless blaze in pursuit.

The car is metal, the conductor thought. *They will be safe,* he assured himself. But what about him? Where could he hide? He looked around and knew immediately that he had no escape. He thought of his wife and children at home. How would they make their living without him? It was a hard enough world, but to be a widow with a half-dozen children and one on the way...

Maybe I should return to the train car? he thought in a panic. The roof of the station suddenly burst into fire and as the flames reached the train car, he heard coughing, and the muffled voices of the women inside, singing a hymn as the children wept and wailed in terror.

Then he saw it looming above him like a barrel on stilts: the water tower. Swiftly tearing his jacket off, he scaled the ladder, climbing as quickly as he could, gripping the rungs with sweating hands. Smoke billowed around him and his eyes watered as the encompassing heat intensified. Clothes smoking, the hairs on his arms singed, he reached the top, tore open the lid and leapt into the water with a splash and felt an immediate feeling of relief.

Gasping for breath, his heart throbbing, Daniel floated in the water and thought of his family. *He would live*, he thought with satisfaction, and his family would not starve. He closed his eyes and smiled at his initiative, and tried to ignore the raging roar of the wildfire surrounding him, as well as the distant shrieks of the women and children, until at last the screams below merged with his own painful screams echoing inside the chamber, as the water within rapidly rose in temperature until it boiled, while beneath him, the steel sanctuary became an oven, baking its innocent inhabitants into unrecognizable piles of charred bone and ash.

CHAPTER FOUR

The two men stood quietly and watched the sun as it descended through the branches in vivid orange streams that sparkled on the crests of the ripples and threw lengthening shadows streaking across the cold gray concrete bridge that spanned the undulating waters of the Paint River. The smaller and older of the two men leaned his frail body on his cane and spoke in a sibilant whisper.

"Have you considered my offer any further, Ethan?" he asked.

"It still is a beautiful town I admit," the younger man said in a deep rumbling voice. "and I'm sure Mary would love it here?"

As he stood watching the river flow past, one noticed an impressive physique under his clothing, especially for a middle-aged man. Handsome, with graying hair, he stood solidly and moved with a natural grace despite his large frame. His square jaw gave him the appearance of a senator or a boxer, and he looked as though he kept active with weight training, and possibly even sparring in the ring.

"I know she would, and it would be a great place for your children and grandchildren to visit," the elderly man's blue eyes sparkled and his few remaining strands of fine white hair fluttered in the light breeze.

"Hunting, fishing, fresh air, peace and quiet… it all sounds too good to be true." The handsome man's eyes followed the arc of a swallow in flight as it veered out from under the shadows of the underside of the bridge and attacked the mosquitoes in the air with joyous abandon. "So what's catch, 'Carl'? Or should I call you Pastor?" he asked with a grin.

"We've known each other far too long for formalities, Ethan," Pastor Carlsson said softly.

"You know, I'll never forget those days back at Lutheran summer camp, when you were my counselor and wrestling coach."

"Yes, you were quite the handful back in those days," the minister said, his eyes moistening as he remembered the smell of pine trees, musty sleeping bags and maple-syrup covered flapjacks for breakfast in the remote and chilly mornings of the far away past.

"You were a big influence on me," the younger man said. "and I've never really thanked you properly for it. You got me started in my career."

"I was just glad to be of assistance. I considered it my duty in those days to help steer young men into constructive directions more beneficial for their youthful and sometimes misguided energies."

"I met Mary in D.C. you know. Best thing that ever happened to me too. Four kids later and she is still a swell egg, still even puts up with moving all the time and traveling all over the world to some pretty unpleasant countries."

"She certainly seems special."

"You don't know the first of it." Ethan pondered, remembering her frightened face at the sound of late night phone calls and her calm demeanor during hurried retreats through airports. "So, she's really into quilting—think she could get involved with any of that around here?"

"Crystal Falls is the quilting capitol of the world."

"Really? I didn't know that."

"It isn't really. I just made that up so you would agree."

They chuckled with good humor as the sun sank further below the horizon, further darkening the atmosphere of the secluded park.

"Well I have to say, Pastor... I have put in my time. The kids are all either off at school or traveling their own paths. I know the agency would probably prefer I lay low in some little podunk town and... No offense intended."

"None taken," the pastor said smiling.

"But heck, Carl—I'm only 50. I still feel pretty darn healthy. What am I going to do? Hunting and fishing are swell, but just sitting around would probably make me crazy after about two weeks."

"That's why I think you should take a job—"

"A job? Here? What kind of job?"

"Nothing much. Nothing you couldn't handle anyway. You see, we have an election upcoming in a few months and—"

"Election?"

"That would give you the time to establish residency, make friends, get a feel for the layout..."

"For what, Town Dog Catcher?" The younger man laughed loudly.

"Actually, I believe what this county needs is a new sheriff," Pastor Carlsson responded quietly.

"Sheriff?"

"Yes."

"But don't you already have a sheriff?"

"We do."

"That fat clown—Junior something—you pointed him out to me when we drove by the Burger Barn."

"That's right."

The big man guffawed. "I'm sorry Carl, but I can't see myself hanging out with Andy and Barney down at Floyd's Barber Shop

14

all day, keeping the town drunk locked up and playing checkers and sipping shakes at the malt shop."

"Oh, I think you would find the job a bit more challenging than that."

"How so?"

The pastor paused and looked at the ground before continuing. His lips trembled as he spoke.

"There is a darkness here."

"Say again?"

"A darkness. An evil. It is all around us and so thick that it seeps into our very souls."

"What are you talking about?"

"The evil one. He is here. I feel his presence. It is a corruption," he hissed.

"Here, in this beautiful place in the middle of nowhere? You have to be kidding. I can't imagine anything worse happening here than the bait shop runs out of minnows, or someone runs a stop sign, maybe a shoplifting kid..."

"How about acid, speed, crack, even heroin?"

"What! In this place?"

"In this place. Drugs, rape, murder..."

"Are you serious?"

The pastor nodded and spoke excitedly. "You don't know what a cesspool it is here beneath it's peaceful surface, Ethan. It is a foul pit leading to the bowels of Hell itself. And the fat man is at the center of it. Nothing is done in this town without his say so. You remove him and we can begin the cleansing and bring light into the darkness once more."

"That tub of lard with mustard on his face chewing down a double-bypass burger? He doesn't seem like he'd be much trouble."

"Don't let his appearance fool you my friend; he is a wolf in sheep's clothing and not an adversary to be taken lightly."

"But if it's so bad, why would you suggest I move here... bring Mary and expose her to danger?"

The pastor sighed heavily and spoke forcibly, his eyes watering.

"There is danger everywhere, Ethan. You know that as well as I do if not more so from your years in the CIA. But we have to... make a stand somewhere. If we don't stop the evil in a place like Crystal Falls, then how can we ever expect to stop it anywhere. It is our moral duty to sacrifice our lives to bring about our Savior's Kingdom here on Earth as best we can. Our rewards will come in Heaven."

"Amen."

"Will you do it, Ethan? If not for me, then for the young people of America—the innocent children in all the small towns across this country who unwittingly are being led astray by the beast. Please, help me save them."

The large man closed his eyes and thought hard before replying at last.

"I'll talk to Mary."

CHAPTER FIVE

In the misty distance, the weary young man could just make out the water tower and the top of the county courthouse from the corner near the edge of town where he was dropped off by the truck driver who gave him a ride over the last several miles. There was no sense trying to hitch another ride across town as traffic was sparse and the few drivers that passed by seemed to be hostile to those unlucky enough to be pedestrians on the road. He would have to walk the final few miles.

Entering into the town itself, he noticed there were a few new buildings erected since he left just over two years ago. A new gas station/convenience store, a half-empty mini-mall, and some new cheap-looking apartments graced the periphery.

Crossing over the Paint River Bridge, he paused and leaned over the railing to stare down into the iron orange-tinted water that steadily proceeded past below him and felt in his heart that he had finally reached his home, imperfect as it was, at last.

Painfully ascending the steep sidewalk along Superior Street, he passed the drug store, the hardware store, the library—but he noticed that more of the storefronts, including the ice cream parlor, were boarded up with for sale signs in the windows.

His legs ached as he arduously mounted the street and made his way closer to the courthouse that stood on the high hill, central to the town. From the courthouse, the three statues of Law, Mercy and Justice looked down as always, watching the return of the prodigal with wary eyes.

Jeremy trudged past his old school and felt a momentary twinge, sadly realizing he had missed the last few years of life. It pained him that he had missed going to school with and graduating with his friends. *Were they still around?* he wondered, *and if so, would they even want to see me again?*

He turned the corner and felt like his feet were leading him down a long forgotten path back to the place where he grew up. His heart began to race and he picked up his pace. He had not seen his mother in nearly a year and had not spoken to her for over a month when she had expressed her joy at his being released soon. There was no way she would simply disappear at this time when she knew he was getting out, even if he did not plan on coming home except perhaps to say goodbye for the last time.

Who knows? Maybe she's come back now and it was all a false alarm. And I can kiss her one last time and say my goodbyes and then hit the road to wherever my fate leads me, he reasoned.

He walked past the older brick home where his step-grandmother, Junior's mom, lived and wondered if the batty old broad was still alive. She must be still kicking as he was pretty sure they would have let him know if she had croaked. She had never been very friendly to him anyway, and he had no desire to stop in and see how she was doing. Two blocks away, he entered a neighborhood of newer ranch houses, most of which were clean and well-maintained. He spotted his destination at the end of the road about a block away and saw the Sheriff's car parked in the driveway and felt the fear and rage swell inside of him.

As he arrived at the house, he was pleased to discover that his rusted old Dodge Dart—a birthday present from his Mom, one he that he barely got to drive before the 'incident,' was parked there as well. *She must have saved it for me all these years*, he thought joyfully, but as he approached even closer, his mood shifted to anger as he saw all his clothes and belongings were dumped in a pile out in the yard.

"What the hell?" he muttered, but he knew at once what was happening.

His car was unlocked, with the keys in the ignition, and so he started picking up his stuff and throwing it in the back seat. The fat man came out when he heard the noise. He had a box of comics and car magazines and threw it down at Jeremy's feet.

"So you're back," he said with a sneer.

"Don't worry, it ain't for long," the boy answered and picked up the box and placed it in the car. "Knew I was coming eh?"

"They gave me a call, let me know you were on your way, and then Stan Jacobson called and said he saw you walking past the hardware store."

"Good ol' Stan. Good to know some things never change."

Jeremy motioned to his clothes and personal items strewn about. "Thanks for getting my stuff together for me."

"You're lucky we kept it," Junior snarled. *He looks older, a little heavier and his curls were grayer*, Jeremy thought.

"You can't stay here, you know," the Sheriff added forcefully with his hands on his gun belt.

"Didn't plan on it. So where's Mom?", Jeremy questioned.

Junior blanched and answered with a curt, "She ain't here."

"I figured that. Even with a prick like you around, she would've been here if she knew I was coming."

"She knew. She's just got other things on her mind right now. She probably took off for a bit to get her head straight or something. You know how moody she is. She was always going for those drives by herself."

Jeremy nodded, remembering, but something still didn't feel right. Junior seemed nervous.

"How long she been gone this time?"

"A few days," he mumbled with a worried look on his face.

"Whoa, that ain't right."

"Naw, it ain't nothing serious. We just had a bit of a dust up."

"About me?"

"What do you think? Was there ever anything else? We could'a had a nice life without you, you little bastard. I tried everything to raise you right, but you still turned out like your daddy. She always let you have your way and look what it got you. And now she's trying to punish me by embarrassing me right before the election."

"How's the election coming?" Jeremy asked. He had seen the signs in yards all across town reminding him of the opportunity to get a dig.

Junior face reddened. "Fuck you."

"Not so good?" Jeremy asked with a chuckle. He was honestly puzzled though; he knew the local elections around here were usually a rubber stamp for the status quo. "Who've they got running against you this time that's got you so worried, a tomato plant?" Jeremy knew the answer, but enjoyed rubbing it in.

"I told you on the phone. Some outsider," Junior snarled. "A goddamn retired CIA agent says he's gonna come in and clean up."

"Oh that's right, you did tell me that. Must have slipped my mind. CIA, huh? No wonder you're worried. So the 'king' has finally met his match? Well long live the new king."

"This thing ain't over yet," the cop growled. "Been plenty of folks make the mistake of underestimating me in the past. This time ain't no different." As Junior's anger surged, the young man's body tensed. He had seen his stepfather's rages plenty of times before, and both experienced and seen the results of his wrath, but now things had changed. His stepdad had gotten plenty of licks in all those years while Jeremy was growing up, especially when Mom wasn't looking. but...*I'd love to see him try it now,* he thought. *Go ahead fat boy, take a poke.*

"But if that ain't all," Junior muttered, "some stupid punk junior high school kid just shot and killed a little girl and is hiding out in the woods somewhere. I got men and dogs looking, but so far it's like he's vanished. Just what I fucking need right now."

"I can imagine dead little girls can be quite an inconvenience." Jeremy taunted. "I suppose this makes you look soft on crime or something."

"And to top it all off, now you show up, of all people."

"Glad to be of service. Sucks to be you, I guess."

Junior ignored his stepson's comments and continued his rant as he quickly headed for his car and climbed in, wedging his hefty body into place. "Take my advice, punk," he called out the window, "and just keep on moving. You just take your worthless piece of junk, sorry excuse for a car, and all your crap, and get the hell out of Crystal Falls. Maybe go south, far south. Keep going until you hit water. Then go some more. I hear Florida is the place for lowlifes like you. I'll tell your mother you stopped by."

"You couldn't pay me to stay in this God-forsaken hellhole any longer than I have to," Jeremy snapped, bending to pick up more of his clothes—which he suddenly realized were all too small for him now. "But I am sticking around until Mom comes back."

"Goddamn it, you do what you want, but mark my word you little jackass, you had better darn well stay the fuck out of my way," Junior shouted before tearing off down the street.

Jeremy shook with rage. Reaching into the car, he pulled out all his old, too-small clothes and threw them back onto the yard. Encountering Junior again had been more disturbing than he had imagined, and he hoped that he would not cross paths with his stepfather again. But he also knew that was probably not going to be the case, and when the confrontation occurred, he would need to be ready for anything.

In the meantime, he had no place to stay and wasn't sure if any of his friends would remember him, or even want to. That, and the thirst he had worked up arguing with the fat man made the decision for him. Like a murderer returning to the scene of the crime, he figured he might as well face the music sooner rather than later, and so he climbed into his car. With a choke and a cloud of blue smoke, the wreck started up, and Jeremy steered it toward the destination where he hoped to find a friend who could offer him a couch or bed: The Lakeside Bar.

CHAPTER SIX

Her back ached as she washed her hands and buttoned up her sweater, while advising the night nurse how crazy the day had been. The crazy, dementia-addled woman on the first floor had somehow gotten out of her room and made it out the front door and nearly into the street. The elderly resident had packed a suitcase full of toilet paper rolls, old newspapers and odd bits of clothing, and put on a party hat left over from a recent birthday celebration, one slipper and a raincoat over her nightgown. Katy caught her just as she was stepping off the curb. The woman smiled broadly as she told Katy that she was on her way to Cleveland to visit her sister—who Katy knew had been dead at least ten years. It had taken considerable effort to get the woman back into her room and medicated enough to sleep soundly, because although the woman's body was paper thin and she only weighed 100 pounds, she was driven as though she were pumped full of adrenaline. *Her brain was unaware*, Katy thought, *but her body knew that she was dying; and it was making a last effort to escape—to escape the fate we all must share.*

Katy shuddered as she thought of herself someday with wrinkled, mottled skin nearly translucent and papery like a manuscript made from feathery birch bark, and blank, confused eyes, seeing before them the shadowy images of the long dead still living in a slowly fading sense of reality. She checked herself in the mirror and was assured that she was still what one might call pretty, with long auburn hair and a pleasing symmetry to her overall appearance. But of course, she knew that her most attractive feature was her big dark eyes, a truly rare feature in a red head, and one that used to lead her uncles to serenade her with *Dark Eyes* on their accordions, much to her embarrassment.

As Katy relayed the day's activities, the night nurse giggled and rolled his eyes, fearing that he may be in for a tumultuous

22

night if the attempted escapee woke up and paced her room ferociously as she often did.

But the adventure with the dementia patient was only part of Katy's day. Two other residents were restless, the burly double-amputee rammed his wheelchair into the wall and shouted obscenities for several hours, while the mute crippled boy in the corner room refused to eat and remained huddled in a fetal position. He was already so thin and sad that Katy felt that he was willing himself to die.

Between the feeding and bathing and therapy and the changing of bedpans and bedding, she was exhausted, both mentally and physically. She would have preferred to simply go home and soak in a hot bath the rest of the night, but she had promised a few girlfriends she would meet them for a couple drinks and some much needed relaxation at the Lakeside.

Katy wasn't really a fan of the place, which was known among the younger residents of the town as a bit of a sleazy "meat market," but it really wasn't all that bad since it had burned down and was rebuilt a few months ago. Previously, the old bar was a disgusting dive frequented by bikers, truckers, hard core drunks and prostitutes and was infamous for the violent fights that broke out among the lowlifes that frequented the place, several of which had resulted in a murder or two. When the old owner died a year ago, his kids took over, and then when a mysterious fire damaged the property six months later, the club was remodeled into a cleaner, friendlier establishment that tried hard to attract a younger crowd. Still too small, with no stage, and with owners too cheap to hire a band, the place instead offered a trusty jukebox filled with most of the hits from the '50s to the present, and a small dance floor where the young folks could dance the night away on the weekends.

A quick drive back to her apartment, a few bites of leftovers to eat and then a shower and quick spiff up her hair and makeup and she could be down to the club in time for what she suspected would be yet another boring night of the same tired jokes and stupid pickup lines from the usual crowd of local boys. Although she knew it would just be more of the same, at least it would be a break from her daily grind. And who knows, maybe someday she'd meet someone special.

Voi avete un cor fedele — a faithful heart, that's what the old man in Room 207 always said, she thought with a chuckle. That's what she needed, he always told her: someone to care for and share her life. He was a funny old bird, OK maybe not that old, but nearly a quadriplegic—with one eye, one ear and a grotesquely scarred face, but he was kind and she liked him best of all her wards. He'd get into some weird moods and quote the Bible some, but it wasn't like he was preaching at her, so she didn't mind too much.

They told her when she started that he was some druggie who crashed his car back in the day. He used give a warning talk about drugs and drinking to all the incoming high school seniors every year when school started—and she remembered when he talked to her class and scared them all nearly to death with his hideous appearance. But they cut that out a couple years ago and—since he didn't have any family or friends around, he was pretty much stuck in his room without any visitors. She felt sorry for him as she seemed to be his only companion and thought that maybe someday she'd take him out to the park to get some fresh air and sunshine, only something always came up and she never got around to it. Maybe this weekend, she thought, but she knew she probably had laundry or something that would prevent her from carrying out her plan.

And as she pulled into the parking lot and ascended the stairs to her apartment, the old man and his funny sayings and horrible face faded from her thoughts and disappeared into the dusty recesses of her mind as she turned the key to her door.

CHAPTER SEVEN

Sweltering in the languid stillness of a hot summer's day, a much younger Deputy "Junior" Pultz parked his car off a back road in a shady spot within a thicket of leafy trees. Inside the car, he leaned back and ran a pudgy hand through his blond curly hair, distractedly wiping the sweat from his brow. Yawning in the heat, he leaned back quietly reading with a serious look on his face. Turning through the pages leisurely, he occasionally snorted and giggled as he studied the pornographic magazine in his lap with rapt attention to its delightful contents.

Suddenly, there was a crackle on the radio and the dispatcher's nasal voice disrupted his peaceful interlude.

"Sorry to bother you, June, but it's your mother again," she said.

"Damn," he snarled and put the magazine aside. "Sorry, Sally; guess you better put her through."

"I don't mind, June. She's just lonely. I think it's nice that you take the time to talk to her so much every day."

"Well, she knows she shouldn't be calling me at work. I've told her that, you know. Oh well, I guess you can put her through now."

The fat man shifted uncomfortably as he prepared himself for the call, when a shrill voice resembling the high-pitched mewl of a recently kicked Siamese cat shattered the airwaves.

"Roy, Roy, are you there?"

"Hello, yes Mother. You have to make this quick. You know I'm working."

"Oh I know you are, but I called to tell you I love you, Roy."

The fat man blushed. "Yes, I love you too, Mother."

"Do you love me, Junior? You don't sound glad to hear from me."

"Of course I do, It's just... You see I'm awfully busy and we just talked two hours ago."

"Well, I just had to tell you something. It's important."

The man listened disinterestedly and turned his attention back to the pages in the discarded magazine.

"Oh, what's that?"

"Well, I thought you should know that she finally did it. She shot him."

Startled, Junior sat up with a jerk. "What's that?"

"I told you she would. He had it coming."

"Now slow down a minute, Mom. Take it from the beginning: who shot who?"

"Morgan, silly."

"Morgan who? Are you alright?"

"Of course I'm alright, why wouldn't I be? I didn't get shot. Are you feeling okay, Roy? Did you eat your bran for breakfast? like a good boy?"

"Yes, I'm just fine, Mother. Now tell me what is going on?"

"Because if you're not feeling well, I could bring some of my prune custard. I know how much you love it and it always seemed to help you when you couldn't go poo-poo."

In the background, Junior heard the dispatcher chuckling and the rage boiled in him.

"Sally, this is a private conversation, if you wouldn't mind. Now Mother who the heck is Morgan?"

"Oh you know. I thought I told you before, but maybe that was someone else I told, but... well she finally did it—went and shot that no good twin brother of hers."

"She shot her brother?"

"Oh yes."

"Is he still alive?"

"Who? Oh yes, the brother, but he's in a coma and the doctors don't know for how long."

"When did this happen... where?"

"A few minutes ago... on my program, of course."

"On your—!"

"Yes right there on the show. Can you imagine? I told you Leonard was no good."

"And Leonard is—?"

26

"Morgan's twin brother. And now Randall is going to blackmail Morgan and she may lose custody of Daphne and—"

"Yes of course Mother. That's just terrible isn't it. These are such dangerous times we live in. Which reminds me, I should get back to—"

Yawning, he stole another glance at his magazine.

"But Junior, that wasn't the only reason I called you—you do remember we have a dance tonight?"

"Yes Mother, of course. I'll be by to pick you up by 6:45 sharp. We discussed this already, two hours ago."

"Well, I want you to wear your blue leisure suit."

"Mother!"

"It looks so nice with my blue dress and hair. We'll be the cutest couple on the dance floor."

"Alright, alright, I'll wear the blue suit, now—"

"She's not coming, is she?"

"Who, Jenny?"

"Yes, your wife."

"Probably not. She's not feeling well again these days. Bad stomach or something."

"Well, that is probably for the best. Especially after the last time."

"Now Mom, I told you that she took some medication for her nausea and had a bad reaction."

"Well, whatever it was, she made quite the scene. Why you practically had to carry her out to the car. And that laughing, my word, she sounded like a crazy person. I have to tell you, the ladies were quite upset."

"Yes, you told me. But you can tell the ladies that Jenny probably won't be joining us again."

"Well, I think that would be for the best, considering."

"Ok, ok. Is that all?"

Distracted, Junior squinted at his magazine to get a better view as he turned the pages.

"Oh, and Esther will be there from Sheboygan. And with her unmarried daughter, Janie."

Junior scowled. "Well, won't that be special. Yes, we will certainly have to be sure we show her a good time, won't we? You do realize I am married."

27

"Oh Junior," she began to weep. "I'm so alone since your father died and then you moved away—"

"Oh no. Please don't cry Mama. You know I'd never leave you alone. And you won't ever leave your little Junior, will you? No never. Yes, I know I moved out of the house, but we're only two blocks away."

He sits up and sets the magazine aside as she continued in a shaky voice.

"Oh Junior, you were always such a good boy. Do you remember that time I dressed you up as Little Orphan Annie and you did that wonderful tap dance routine and you sang that beautiful song?"

"How could I forget?"

"I know the other children mocked you, but they were just jealous of your talent."

"Yes, I know."

"You have such a lovely voice. Sing it for me, Roy. Sing that song again."

"No Mom. No. I'm not going to."

Junior's mother sobs.

"No, don't cry. Please Mama don't. Ok Ok, I'll do it."

He takes a deep breath and... starts singing.

"Tomorrow, tomorrow— There, is that what you wanted?"

Giggling is heard on the line.

"Damn it Sally!"

A red sports car with two teenagers in it suddenly sped past. Junior huffs, aggravated that he can't go after them.

"Now Mama. Yes Mama. Yes. I'm your good little boy. But I really should get back to work. Yes, it's a very important case. Yes, I'm sure Dad would be proud. Yes, I know he was already the county sheriff when he was my age and I'm still just a deputy. Yes, he was a great man and I miss him too."

He snarls and punches the dashboard.

"Now I really have to go. Oh, the show is back on. That's good. No don't call me back. You can tell me tonight what happens to Victor and Lucy who are trapped in the old mine. Yes, we'll talk then. I won't be late."

He beats his head against the steering wheel.

"Hello Mom?"

No response.

"She's hung up, Junior."

"Thanks Sally, thanks a lot."

"Aw she is so cute, and her son is such a singer. My heart is still fluttering."

"You tell anyone about this and—"

"Don't worry, I won't say a word… Annie."

"Arrrr!!!"

Sally 's laugh faded as she disconnected. With a snarl, Junior picked up the magazine and went back to his reading. His interest was taken in by a page he turned to in the book hidden inside of the pornographic magazine. He smiled to himself as he studied the page of the *Anarchist's Cookbook* featuring a detailed diagram of how to build a bomb.

CHAPTER EIGHT

Abruptly the late 1891 summer sky darkened from it's morose cinereal coloring, formed itself into colossal crepuscular clouds of black vapor, rumbled its threatening voice loudly over the terrain in bursts and intermittently flashed jagged branches of light vertically through the heavy air. Sharp shafts of lightning spiked, stabbing the parched ground, generating a tiny spark that burst forth and ignited within a dry brushy meadow. Crackling with increasing vitality, the flickering combustion greedily fed upon the desiccated stalks and timber, rapidly swelling into an immense blaze that rose up and out and spread across the territory with increasing violence.

Swept forward by the winds, the flames screamed across the landscape like a howling storm of hellish, tormented ghosts, scorching forest and savanna alike, exuding an intense hot breath and thick mane of smoke. Its malevolent glare arose in the distance like the glowing eyes of a fearsome beast appearing suddenly in the dark depths of a primeval cave. Its' insatiable hunger consumed everything within the swift embrace of its terrible passage, leaving only smoking remnants of copses of trees, miles of smoldering grasslands, the charred skeleton frames of houses and other buildings, and the ashy remains of deer, rabbits, foxes and other animals unable to outrun the ferocious velocity of the fire which surged forward relentlessly—a great tidal wave of conflagration across the prairie.

Even the man-made metal buildings and bridges and the mighty iron horse were not immune to the intensity of the heat, and several human lives had already been lost seeking refuge in vain. Several farms were razed to nothingness, with whole families and livestock seared and choking and devoured by the rapacious inferno. Still unsatisfied, the fire now rushed with destructive eagerness toward the small mining community of Mansfield, Michigan.

The terror of the community could be seen in the eyes of every man, woman and child, as Adele took a breath from her labor—filling buckets from the well, and watched in fear as the citizens of the mining community scurried around frantically. Most of the inhabitants had immediately answered when the alarms rang and had worked energetically together to save the property of the community. Houses, the store, the saloon and the church, the new school, and most importantly of course, the mine, were in danger of utter destruction and had to be protected at all cost.

Adele's father was with a group of men working nonstop down near the mine, because if the mine were destroyed, Adele knew there would be no town. The mine owned the town and employed most of the men who lived there. They owned the houses and the miners and their families paid rent to the company for the shacks they called home.

The pretty red-haired girl had been looking forward to attending the new school that was recently built—her wild brothers had not, and she trembled at the thought that the school might be burned. She loved reading and learning and wished they would save it first, but she also knew that without her father's job at the mine, they would have neither house nor food on the table, so she prayed silently for her father's success in stopping the advance of the flames.

The women had formed a line whose primary purpose was to fill and carry buckets of water from the wells to where the water was needed the most, and they had enlisted several of the smaller children, many who were exhausted with tears streaming down their face, in this task. The older boys helped the men in digging and clearing the firebreak and the moving and stacking of material to try to block the path of the wildfire.

The flames suddenly swerved carried along by a shift in the wind and attacked the Henderson farm on the edge of town, quickly turning the wooden farmhouse into a glowing bonfire. The men from the town ran toward the home with the horse drawn water tank galloping along.

Ignoring the shouts of her mother, Adele hurried off through the grass and mud to the Henderson barn to warn the family. Old Mr. Henderson was a strange one, a religious zealot who preached that the town of Mansfield was a modern Sodom. He was the only male member of the town who had not heeded the call for help, but who instead herded his swine, his young wife and two daughters into the barn, where they barricaded themselves inside and uttered loud prayers for salvation. Adele had formed a bit of a friendship with the shy girls and had looked forward to reading stories to the younger girls in school in preparation for her future dream of becoming a schoolteacher.

"Mr. Henderson," she screamed and pounded on the locked barn door with her fist. Inside, she could hear the girls crying and Mr. Henderson reading out loud from the Bible in an authoritative voice.

Adele pleaded, "Mr. Henderson please! The fire is almost here. Please come out!"

From within, she heard the man gruff voice shouting "It is the judgement of the Lord!" and the shrill screams of the girls and the squealing of frightened swine coming from the barn.

"Addy, come away," she heard her father call.

The men and women struggled to put out the flaming farmhouse, but to no avail, and the fire moved quickly toward the barn. Then suddenly, the wind shifted again and the blaze raced off to the distance, leaving the barn untouched.

As the men ran back to their work on another firebreak before the fire could reach the mine, Adele ran back and pounded on the door of the barn and shouted. "It missed you, Mr. Henderson. It's a miracle. You can come out now." But the answer was only one of silence. Adele longed to comfort the girls, but the door was locked tightly, and her mother called her away to help carry water.

Several hours later, when at last the fire receded and the danger was past, the concerned men of the town broke down the doors to the barn, and found Henderson dead of a gunshot wound to the head, his body covered with blood and slumped in a heap in the center of the room, his blood-stained Bible still open to Revelations. In the shadows of the barn, the pigs were found slaughtered, while his wife and daughters' bodies were discovered neatly stacked in separate corners, their throats cut from ear to ear.

CHAPTER NINE

Therefore I hated life; because the work that is wrought under the sun is grievous unto me: for all is vanity and vexation of spirit. I am a brother to dragons, and a companion to owls. My soul is weary of my life.

Another day. Or is it night? No, day. But morning or evening? So many days, nights, mornings, evenings, yet nothing seems to change.

The man that wandereth out of the way of understanding shall remain in the congregation of the dead.

Am I dead? Am I alive. It's all the same. Am I cursed? Am I blessed?

Sorrow is better than laughter: for by the sadness of the countenance the heart is made better.
For all his days are sorrows, and his travail grief; yea, his heart taketh not rest in the night.
For God shall bring every work into judgment, with every secret thing, whether it be good, or whether it be evil.

It has been my fate to be confined to this bed for so many long years, staring at the cracks in the ceiling and measuring their lengths with my eyes as they grow longer ever so perceptibly. I estimate they have increased by nearly an inch and a half in the many years or more that I have been imprisoned here. My repentance is honest, yet my punishment continues relentlessly and for good measure, I expect you would agree.

That which is crooked cannot be made straight. For wrath killeth the foolish man, and envy slayeth the silly one.

I have television. I have books on tape. The Bible on tape. I have no friends and few visitors. I have only the madness in my mind.

For the arrows of the Almighty are within me, the poison whereof drinketh up my spirit: the terrors of God do set themselves in array against me.

But what is this? I see that I am visited by a little spider. His hairy legs grip the wall and he climbs slowly, cautiously, pausing for minutes at a time, unaware that I couldn't get up and smash him even if I wanted to. I watch his movement across the wall and amuse myself with predicting his next maneuver. Oh stay a while, won't you? Keep a lonely soul company. But as I watch, he slips behind the picture on the wall — Turner's *"The Battle of Trafalgar — as seen from the Mizen Starboard Shrouds of the Victory."* This beautiful and tragic picture whose chaotic and claustrophobic depiction of the battle and noble death of Admiral Nelson I have examined with rapt attention and in great detail for what seems a lifetime. I have come to hate that picture.

So am I made to possess months of vanity, and wearisome nights are appointed to me.
When I lie down, I say, When shall I arise, and the night be gone? and I am full of tossings to and fro unto the dawning of the day.
My flesh is clothed with worms and clods of dust; my skin is broken, and become loathsome.
My days are swifter than a weaver's shuttle, and are spent without hope.
O remember that my life is wind: mine eye shall no more see good.
The eye of him that hath seen me shall see me no more: thine eyes are upon me, and I am not.
As the cloud is consumed and vanisheth away: so he that goeth down to the grave shall come up no more.

He shall return no more to his house, neither shall his place know him any more.

Therefore I will not refrain my mouth; I will speak in the anguish of my spirit; I will complain in the bitterness of my soul.

It has been more than fifteen years since the terrible events that determined my fall into a living nightmare. My ascendance from cowardly nobody to becoming one of the worst and most feared drug dealers in the area: the man known as the Preacher, who helped cover up murders, sent others to death, threatened countless others, sold poison to children, killed his best friend... and buried him in a pit. Stole my best friend's woman, and... nearly killed her in a car crash that killed our daughter and placed me deservedly into this.... rotting cell.

And now my soul is poured out upon me; the days of affliction have taken hold upon me.

My bones are pierced in me in the night season: and my sinews take no rest.

By the great force of my disease is my garment changed: it bindeth me about as the collar of my coat.

He hath cast me into the mire, and I am become like dust and ashes.

I cry unto thee, and thou dost not hear me: I stand up, and thou regardest me not.

Thou art become cruel to me: with thy strong hand thou opposest thyself against me.

Thou liftest me up to the wind; thou causest me to ride upon it, and dissolvest my substance.

For I know that thou wilt bring me to death, and to the house appointed for all living.

Death would be a mercy. A cool drink of pure stream water within the searing heat of a desert.

I am the man that hath seen affliction by the rod of his wrath.

He hath led me, and brought me into darkness, but not into light.

Surely against me is he turned; he turneth his hand against me all the day.

My flesh and my skin hath he made old; he hath broken my bones.

He hath builded against me, and compassed me with gall and travail.

He hath set me in dark places, as they that be dead of old.

He hath hedged me about, that I cannot get out: he hath made my chain heavy.

Also when I cry and shout, he shutteth out my prayer.

I am alone save for one unwanted visitor who comes torment me and oppress me with my guilt.

He hath turned aside my ways, and pulled me in pieces: he hath made me desolate.

I am in pain.

CHAPTER TEN

When the boy emerged from the woods and sauntered lazily toward the cabin, the old women could hardly believe her eyes, and she had a brief moment where her heart stirred and she hoped Jim had come back from the war after all—that it had all just been one terrible joke played on her by the Army and that maybe he didn't get blown to bits in a valley in Viet Nam like they told her after all. But then she realized that her Jim was heavier and walked differently and, as the boy came closer, she could see this kid was too young and skinny to be her long dead son.

She stopped hanging the laundry on the line and watched with a wary eye as Tim approached across the meadow appearing restless and apprehensive.

"You lost, boy?" she challenged.

There was no response as the boy moved forward toward her, his eyes toward the ground.

"Ain't you supposed to be in school?" she asked, to no response.

"Playing hooky huh? My Jim used to do that and go squirrel hunting. Is that what you're doing?"

The young man advanced quietly.

"Well, come on in. You look like you could use a bite to eat."

The boy looked up and shook his head in affirmation.

She turned to go inside, and called over her shoulder. "Quiet one, ain't ya? You can leave your gun outside on the porch, and take them muddy boots off too, I just done the floors."

The boy followed her, as she continued speaking. Lord knows it had been some time since she had spoken to anyone, let alone had a visitor. Days for sure, maybe weeks—she wasn't real sure. She kept her house spotless in case a visitor arrived, but there had been no one in quite some time. She was alone and the silence of the woods surrounding her home suddenly rushed in on her and she was made acutely aware of her isolation.

"I got some cold soda pop in the fridge," she rattled on nervously, "and you can watch some TV—I ain't had it on in some days 'cause I don't watch it much and it don't get much of a picture and on account of my hearing—I don't hear too good anymore."

The boy did not answer, but stopped and stood silently watching her move slowly toward her front door.

"There ain't nothing much to watch anymore anyway. Just a bunch of sex and killing—blood and guts all over the place. I can't stand it. I like things kept clean. You take them boots off, ok?"

She stepped up the first step with difficulty, still speaking as if to herself.

"I suppose you like all that stuff in the TV and movies. The young folks always do. But me, I had enough of it. My boy was just a bit older than you, and he got all hopped up on that shooting and killing and look what it got him. Can't even bear to think about his body all chopped up in pieces and burned up over in that stinking jungle. My husband was so broken up about it, he didn't last much more than a year after. Made himself so sick drinking and smoking so as to die and leave me alone out here. Terrible thing to watch, him just wasting away and coughing up blood and then the hacking and gasping and rattling when he went."

She took the second step shakily and she felt the presence behind her move closer.

"Don't suppose you ever saw anyone die yet. You're too young. But you'll learn, like we all do. It's a part of nature. The old gotta go so the young can live. It's just a shame when it's a young person that gets killed. But the old ones, well they've lived long enough I guess."

A click behind her as she ascended the final step. She heard it loud and clear— despite her hearing, and recognized the sound from her husband and son's hunting days years ago.

"You know the movies I like are the old ones, the ones in black and white. You ever seen any of those? There ain't no killing—or maybe just a murder or something that happens but you don't actually see it—it's all off-screen. I like it if there ain't no blood. I used to kill chickens for my husband, but I got sick of it, especially after the boy died. I don't like blood—all that sticky mess to clean up. Yes sir, I like to keep things clean. You'll remember those boots won't you?"

She could feel the boy's eyes on her back as she rambled on. "But those old movies, I still watch them sometimes. I can't hear much of what they are saying, but I love the pictures, though they make me kind happy and sad at the same time. You know what I mean? They take me back to when I was your age. I used to save up my money, it was only a dime you know, but that was hard to come by in those days, and I'd go with my girlfriends and watch the actresses on the screen and pretend we were them—all dressed up in those fancy gowns and dresses and pearls and we'd swoon over those actors—they were all so handsome in their suits and ties, not dressed like those bums are nowadays. I just loved the way they used to dance across the floor just like they were flying. Of course all those actors and actresses are long dead now, all my friends too. You'll know what that's like someday, if you're one of the lucky ones."

The silence persisted. She opened the door without looking back.

"You're probably all worn out from all your hiking around so you just come on in and sit on the sofa and we'll call your folks to come and get—"

A crack. She felt searing pain as her legs gave way and her body slumped down in the entryway, sticky red spurting onto her clean floor. *Damn,* she thought bitterly, *who will clean the mess up?* But as the blackness came, she thought she heard... Was that Jim she heard calling for his mother from the depths of a jungle forest?

The boy dutifully removed his boots before he stepped over the body in the doorway.

CHAPTER ELEVEN

It's one of these nights, another Saturday night, and the place is filled with the silhouettes of the lonely, only the lonely, all the lonely people, escaping their lonely days, free fallin' in their throes of self pity, their careless whispers barely registering over the loud electronic pulses throbbing like a heartbeat through my vibrating membranes.

Are you lonesome tonight?

Oh lonesome me

I get lonely

Nobody wants to be lonely

Apparently the entities that continue to feed me with their silver coins—punching my buttons, forcing me to produce pleasurable sound waves for their entertainment like a subservient minstrel in a chaotic medieval court—subscribe to a belief that it takes two to be happy together. And as such, they are once again in the wild night that is calling and livin' the vida loca. Don't worry, be happy, it isn't the eve of destruction. Yet.

So they gather in the darkness under neon lights and play their games because it's all in the game, a foolish game, wicked game. And the name of the game is...

Love
The Game of Love.
Sweet Love
Crazy in Love

Whole Lotta Love

All those Silly Love Songs

Words Of Love
You Can't Hurry Love
Baby I Need Your Lovin'
Love the One You're With
I Was Made To Love Her
Love Her Madly
To Love Somebody
Fallin' In Love
Love Train
Everlasting Love
Love Is A Many Splendored Thing
Love Me Tender
April Love
Young Love
Crazy Love
Bye Bye Love
(Will You Love Me Tomorrow?)
Love To Love You Baby
Love Is Alive
I'd Really Love To See You Tonight
She Loves You
I Feel Love
And I Love Her
All My Loving
Fooled Around and Fell in Love
Love Will Find A Way
Crazy Little Thing Called Love
Endless Love
The Power of Love
I Want To Know What Love Is
Is This Love?
Can You Feel the Love Tonight?
Show Me Love
Now and Forever
Forever in Love

So Much in Love
100% Pure Love
Baby, I Love Your Way
If You Had my Love
Young Love
Secret Love
I Will Always Love You
When A Man Loves A Woman
What's Luv?

With all this L-O-V-E in the air, how can anyone resist? The Boy enters nonchalantly and approaches the bar. The Girl eyes him with a sidelong glance.

His long straggly hair hangs down over his eyes that dart back and forth nervously as if searching for someone familiar. He orders a beer, surveys the room and asks the bartender what happened to the crappy old bar he used to sneak into.

The girl giggles at a joke she has only half heard that one of her girlfriends has shouted across the table to her. Her black eyes meet his cold grey ones and...

Cupid pull back your bow....

The liquid refreshment adds to the ambience. The girls order another round and dance with each other. The boys drink shots and arm wrestle.

Do you like Pina Coladas?
Gimme a Gin and Juice
Tequila

How Do you Talk to an Angel? He thinks looking at the dark-haired beauty whose smile invites kissing.

I'm Your Angel She thinks, dreaming of his strong arms and confident eyes.

My Special Angel
Angel
Angel of Mine
Angel, Angel, Angel

So the wheels spin producing electricity and the magnetism takes hold and the attraction pulls the bodies closer and they approach each other slowly, but unstoppably, and before you know it it's "Good Golly Miss Molly meet Johnny B. Goode." Just like Jack and Diane, both refugees from Heartbreak Hotel and looking for someone to un-break their hearts.

And he saw her standing there and
Mercy, Mercy, Mercy!!!
I've Got to Get You Into My Life because you Light My Fire
And you lift me Higher And Higher
I'm All Shook Up
You are so Beautiful
I Want To Hold Your Hand

He's a king of the road, a lonely bull, an alley cat, a daydream believer, a hero (Billy, don't be a hero), a Kung Fu Fighter, hot blooded but as cold as ice.

And she thinks "he's so fine, come a little bit closer"

And he's picking' up good vibrations like a message in a bottle from a genie in a bottle.

"Hello it's me," he begins.
"Oh, Boy!" she smiles, her heart pounding.

"I haven't seen you around before," she says. "Where are you from?"
"I hate to admit that I'm from Crystal Falls. Just been away for a bit,"
"You look kinda familiar, did you go to school here?"
"Yeah, I was supposed to graduate in '02, but plans kinda got changed."

"I was class of '00 - The Millennials"

"I'm surprised I don't remember you. I like older women," he says with an adorable grin. She blushes.

"I'm Katja—Katy Randala," she puts out her hand.

"Oh yeah, now I remember." She looked good then; she looks even better now. "I'm Jeremy…" he starts. "Um… Hawkins." He takes her hand and feels the warmth and softness that sends an electric current through his body.

"I remember you," she says. "You—" she pulls her hand away startled.

"Yeah, that was me."

'You're Junior's son."

"Don't even say that. I ain't related one bit to that prick."

"But…"

"My mom's married to him—that's all."

"They let you out already? After you—"

"Hey, it was an accident and I was a minor, so they couldn't keep me in any longer. I'm headed out West to maybe work on an oil rig or something. I just came back to say 'bye' to my mom."

He's a rebel, a wild thing, crazy, she thinks.

And he agrees and adds: I fought the law and I shot the sheriff (or would like to anyway).

And she knows he's a sweet talkin' guy, a smooth operator, a travelin' man, a ramblin' man, but oh what'a man!

She could be Amanda, Peggy Sue, Sara, Kyrie, Cecelia, Gloria, Rosanna, Proud Mary, Mustang Sally, Little Susie, but she's just Katy and he says:

Oh, Pretty Woman, Diamond Girl, Brown…er Black—Eyed Girl, Summer Girl, Party Doll, Rag Doll, Heartbreaker, Sweet Little Rock n' Roller, Dancin'Queen, Maneater, You Sexy Thing, She's got Legs (and knows how to use them), Little Darlin,' Poor Little Fool, The Most Beautiful Girl in the World

And:

You've got Temptation Eyes, and the First Time I Ever I Saw
Your Face
My Eyes Adored You...Your Dark Eyes, Sad Eyes, Hungry
Eyes, Bette Davis Eyes, I Only Have Eyes For You, I Can't Take
My Eyes Off You

"Oh, you're just Jive Talkin" she says, but she's secretly
pleased and he rambles on:

Hey Good Lookin'
Honey
Hey Baby
Be My Baby
Don't Worry Baby
Ruby Baby
My Baby
Baby Blue
Dream Baby
Dream Lover
All You Have to Do is Dream

And as the evening deepens, he wants to get to know her, if he
could. He wants to touch her. He wants to see her move and feel
her in his arms. So he puffs up his chest and takes charge and
boldly goes forth and says let's...

Get the Party Started
Right Here, Right Now
I'm Down 4 U
Listen to the Music
You Make Me Feel Like Dancing
I Hope You Dance
Get Ur Freak On
Do You Wanna Dance?
Let's Dance
You Should Be Dancing
I Wana Sex You Up
Gonna Make You Sweat

Twistin' The Night Away
Doin' the Crocodile Rock

Two bodies enter the dance floor and spin and whirl and touch
gently, achingly breaking, like waves against each other's shore.

And Katy ponders:

What a Girl Wants
All That She Wants
Girls Just Want To Have Fun
 A real Slim Shady with a
Slow Hand and an easy touch
Nice and Slow
Kisses Sweater Than Wine
I Want it That Way
A Cowboy to Take Me Away
I Want to Fly Away
Don't Be Cruel
Don't Bring Me Down
Don't Go Breaking My Heart
I give you a Piece of my Heart
My Achy Breaky Heart
Take My Breath Away
Touch Me In The Morning
because She Needs Someone to Hold Her When She Cries

He wants to be her man. She wants to be his woman. I've seen
it all before. So many times. So many ways. It's always the same:
the two separate souls must merge to become one, to become
whole. They fumble and tease and press harder into one another as
her jealous girlfriends and his rival suitors look on in awe and
envy.

And he sighs with longing

Hold Me Now
Dancing In The Dark
Bump n' Grind

Crazy For You
Can't Fight This Feeling
If You Could Read My Mind
How Sweet It Is
Your Body is a Wonderland
Wonderful Tonight
Fallin'
How Much I Feel
I Want You….
…and I want you to want me too
I'm A Believer
Shout
You Really Got Me
I Only Want To Be With You
Mad About You
Head Over Heels
Girl, You Know It's True
With Every Beat of my Heart
I Want You, I Need You, I Love you

The voices are recognizable: the velvety warbling of Eddy
Arnold, Michael Bolton, Patsy Cline, Don Henley, Prince, Roy
Orbison, Madonna. The pulsating rhythms and melodious timbres
crafted beautifully to persuade the timid and unwilling to sacrifice
their hearts at the altar of the dark God of Love.

And she sighs with longing. And he starts to feel something
he's never felt before: a validation of his being, a connection with
someone, a promise of what life could have to offer. And he goes
on, because most lyrics are written from the male perspective.

Stand By Me
She Believes In Me
Something to Believe In
Reason to Believe
Believe
Because of You
I'd do it All For You
Follow You Down

49

Crazy for this Girl
Make It With You
Go All The Way

Then he sees something in her eyes and

I saw the Sign
Whoomp, There it is

Then He Kissed Me

Eyeless, I can only sense their lips pressed together softly for the first time, as a thousand volcanos explode in their chests sending propulsive convulsions of shockwaves through their entire internal universe.

The boy and girl, or should I say man and woman, leave together and I feel sadness—although tears at this point would rust my metal casing, and they have already suggested replacing me with karaoke machine on Tuesday Nights, but I so long to understand these human feelings and I Don't Wanna Miss A Thing.

As an experienced observer, I am very conscious of the usual progressions that are followed after the initial night of love:

Peaceful Easy Feeling
Morning After
Sundown
Suspicion
I Fall to Pieces
Quit Playing Games With My Heart
Do You Really Want To Hurt Me
Everybody Plays the Fool
Ain't No Sunshine
He'll Have to Go
Release Me
Hit The Road Jack
End of World

Ain't That A Shame
Faded Love
Bye Bye Love
It's a Heartbreak

And finally

Crying

The players will return; they always will; perhaps not the same ones, but they will play the same parts. Every night, long after my metal shell corrodes and their fleshy one crumbles into dust in the wind, their eternal dance will persist in an endless recurring coda of piercing sadness and marvelous bliss.

CHAPTER TWELVE

Junior's pleasant reverie in the shade is abruptly broken by the same sports car with the teenagers in it that flew by earlier zooming past again, this time in the opposite direction

"Damn it!" he said and, stuffing the book and magazine under his seat, he turned on his flashing lights and put the car into gear as he took off in pursuit, sending a spray of rocks and dirt into the air as he pulled out. Turning on his siren, he pursued the speeding car. down a deserted back country road until at last the Camaro pulled over.

Junior lifted his pudgy body out of his car and after approaching the sports car cautiously, he rapped his knuckles on the driver's side window.

A pimply-faced teenaged boy in the driver's seat opened his window.

"Did I do something wrong, officer?" he asked with a smirk.

"License and registration." Junior replies in his best *Dragnet*-style, no nonsense voice.

"I asked you what I did wrong," the boy countered.

"I heard you, and I'm not telling you again," the cop growled. "License and registration."

The kid handed out his license to Junior, who eyed it closely. The driver and the second teen, a weedy kid with spiked hair and a skull tattoo giggled as they dug through the glove compartment unsuccessfully.

"I can't seem to find the registration," the boy tittered. "But it's my car."

"Pretty nice car," Junior muttered. "You don't look like you could afford it. How do I know you didn't steal it?"

"His dad bought it for him," the second teen interjected. "For his birthday."

"I didn't ask you, did I?" Junior snapped, giving the second kid an evil glare. Turning again to the driver, he continued: "Driving a little fast today don't you think?"

"No! Was I? I don't think so."

The second teen burst out laughing.

Junior drummed his fat fingers on the roof and continued thoughtfully.

"Yup. A little fast I think."

"Just testing the engine. There's nobody out on this road anyway."

"Think I saw your friend throw some garbage on the road back there too."

"What? You're crazy. Jim did you do that?" Jim shook his head and guffawed. "See he didn't do it."

Junior stepped back and assumed a gunfighter-like stance with both hands on his belt.

"Looked like a beer can to me. Where do you boys do your shopping? Down at the Mini Mart? We had a report of a couple kids shoplifting some beer there. You fellows kind of fit the description."

The driver erupts in mock rage. "That's bullshit. We didn't steal nothing. Look are you going to give us a ticket or what? We got places to be."

Junior closed his eyes and thought hard.

"A ticket, yes." he said under his breath.

"Just hurry it up if you are going to give it to us, do it, already. My ol' man will take care of it anyway."

"Yeah, you know who his old man is?" The second boy blurted out venomously.

Junior thought about it. Closing his eyes, he remembered a summer day: Ten-year-old Junior playing in the woods. He bends down and floats a "boat" made from a leaf down a creek. Smiling and happy in the sunshine, he follows it downstream.

Looking up, he sees a cabin with some cars parked outside. One of the cars is a sheriff's car. He recognizes it and calls out.

Dad?

Approaching the cabin, he calls again for his father. He walks up onto the porch and tries to look through the window but cannot see. He hears laughter coming from a rear bedroom, so he walks around to the back to where the sounds are coming from. Wiping the filth off the glass with his sleeve, he presses his face against the bedroom window and peers inside.

Within the room, he sees his father with a group of men sitting around half-dressed. They laugh and pass a bottle around. Junior's eyes strive to focus on the shadowy inhabitants of the scene, many of whom he recognizes as friends of his father and prominent townspeople. He studies the group wondering what they are doing, when he suddenly notices the woman bound and gagged on the bed, her eyes wide with terror.

Junior screams.

His father looks up and sees him. His face contorts in rage. Junior turns and runs away, but his father emerges out of the cabin and pursues his son. Huffing, Junior nearly reaches the tree line before his father catches him.

You little son of a bitch!

Junior struggles to escape the man's grasp.

No, Dad!

The Sheriff's belt slashes through the air again across Junior's back. Closing his eyes, he howls in pain.

Junior slowly shook his head from side to side as he awoke from his terrible daydream nightmare. He refocused and spoke softly but firmly to the boys in the car.

"Step out of the car."

"What for?" the pimply youth whined.

Junior felt the rage rising, but maintained his control.

"I said step out of the car."

"OK OK."

The teens snickered as the driver opened the door and climbed out. He was even smaller and skinnier than he looked behind the wheel, but he was dressed in expensive clothes and crossed his arms defiantly while giving Junior a look of bemused disdain.

Junior smiled placidly and asked, "So boys, are you holding?

The boy tittered, "What do you mean?"

"You know what I mean.

"What did he say?" the kid in the passenger seat called.

"He wants to know if I'm 'holding.'"

"Yeah, maybe holding your dick."

The two teens roared with laughter. Junior remained impassive.

"I'm going to have to ask you to empty your pockets."

"No way. I'm pretty sure you need a search warrant for that."

"Empty your pockets."

"I think I want to talk to my dad."

"Yeah, let him call his dad. You like your job, pig? You'll be lucky to find work sweeping up after the elephants once he gets done with you."

Junior smile faded. He shifted his bulky body and spoke grimly.

"Are you resisting arrest?" he asked.

"What?"

"Are you deaf as well as stupid? I asked if you were resisting arrest."

The boy looked startled.

"I didn't know I was being arrested," he stammered. "You can't just arrest me without a reason."

"Oh, I've got a reason. Do you want to hear my reason?"

"What?"

"Come here and I'll tell you."

The young man cautiously leaned in closer to the deputy.

"So what—?"

Exploding into action, Junior yanked out his wooden baton and clubbed the boy violently over the head, knocking him to his knees. The boy's eyes rolled back in his head and blood splattered the side panel of the car as Junior beat him over and over, screaming, "Is this a good enough reason for you?"

The boy in the passenger seat gasped in shocked realization, jumped out of the car and ran frantically into the woods. Junior stopped hitting the driver and left him bleeding and unresponsive on the ground and followed the second boy. Gliding quickly through the underbrush, down the rocky paths he knew well, he chased the second teen down, and proceeded to beat the boy repeatedly with his club until the boy stopped crying for help and lay limp and still in a lifeless heap.

A few minutes later, Junior emerged from the trees. Huffing and puffing noisily behind the red Camaro, he pushed the car forward and downhill along a dirt trail. Sweating heavily in his blood-soaked uniform—the adrenaline still coursing through his system, he pushed the car to the edge of a rise and paused. Taking one last look at the broken and bloody bodies of the boys carefully arranged in the front seat, Junior gave the car a strong final shove —sending it rolling down the slope and into a pond, where it sank slowly beneath the stagnant muddy water.

The sun was low on the horizon as Junior pulled up to his mother's house and climbed hastily out of his cruiser. Dressed in a too-tight, pale blue leisure suit, with shiny black shoes and his hair piled high and perfectly coifed, he carried a duffle bag over his shoulder as he marched forward. Spotting his arrival through the lacy curtains, his mother burst out of the front door dressed to the Ts in a '50s-style blue dress, a gaudy string of fake pearls, a crocheted shawl and freshly-blued hair. She carried a chocolate cake in both hands and chattered away breathlessly.

"Oh, there you are at last, Junior. Why are you so late? I was so worried. I thought we might miss the first dance. Esther is probably already there. You know there is a cake walk. And I promised to help serve the punch."

"Now don't you worry, Mother. Your date has arrived and I'll have you to the dance in a jiffy."

He patiently opened the door to his mother's Caddy and helped her into the passenger seat, placed the cake safely in the back seat and gently buckled her in.

"Now just wait here a moment and I'll be right back."

"Do you have to go to the potty, Dear," she asked brightly. "Don't forget to spray air freshener if you do number two."

Junior winced.

"No Mom, I just have some laundry to do."

"Oh, let me take care of that for you," she squawked and tried to climb back out of the car. Junior hugged her tight and forcefully pushed her back inside.

"No Mom, you just sit tight and relax and let me take care of this. I just got my uniform a little dirty at work."

As he hurried away, she called after him in a shrill voice, "Don't forget that there's fabric softener on the top shelf."

"Thank you, Mother," he replied with a wave as he carried the duffle bag into the house.

He's such a good boy, she thought and wondered what color dress Mrs. Randala would be wearing tonight.

CHAPTER THIRTEEN

Where am I?

I struggle to awaken as though emerging from a dense fog. It is dark. I am cold. I am in pain and I think I am bleeding.

I try to move but I can't. My arms are tied. I am restrained.

I shift and feel a sharp pain that shoots through my body like lightning. I cry out. My face is bruised and I think my leg is broken.

My vision is blurred and my head hurts so bad. I am confused. Who has done this? Who would want to hurt me?

Was it Junior? Or someone else?

I can't remember anything.

I will sleep now and then I will remember.

CHAPTER FOURTEEN

Carrying a basket with some flour and molasses homeward, Adele swished her apron from side to side as she skipped down the dirt street, pretending that she was wearing one of the ball gowns worn by the fancy ladies in the pictures in the general store. There was a dance coming up in a few months and she hoped to be able to attend now that she was fourteen.

Suddenly she heard a boyish giggle and spotted Johnny Randala spying on her from behind one of the wagons parked on the road. Her face reddened. Johnny was a Finnish boy a year older than her, who had been in school with her until he quit to work in the mines a few months ago. He worked the night shift and was probably on his way to work.

"Shut your mouth and stop peeking at me, Johnny Randala," she snapped out of embarrassment. Johnny had been one of the boys—along with her brothers, who always used to tease her about her long skinny legs and freckles. He had always been a pest, but lately he had grown taller than her; his body was broader and more muscular and his attitude more serious. Working at the hard physical labor with the men had changed him, and she was surprised to see that he almost seemed to have become a man.

Of course, she had changed too. She knew she was becoming a woman and was excited, but frightened by it. She had seen firsthand the pain her mother experienced with every birth, as well as with the loss of her children to the flu and pox. Adele had lost two brothers and a sister and had learned that it was a woman's lot to work hard, cry and suffer. Yet, despite the pain she felt compelled to perform her duty, emulate her mother and become a wife and mother.

Johnny jumped out from his hiding place—his long arms and legs moving rapidly, and began walking in step beside her. Adele felt his presence next to her, but tried to ignore him. His gray eyes sparkled as he smiled at her and doffed his soft mining cap. He carried a handkerchief in the other hand which she knew contained the beef and turnip pasty that would be his dinner.

"I am sorry if I frightened you, Miss Adele," he said with a shy smile. "I almost didn't recognize you."

"I don't know what you mean," Adele growled, but she secretly smiled inside.

"I mean…" Johnny paused, searching for the right words. His parents still spoke only Finnish and he struggled to overcome his accent. "Well, may I walk you home?"

"I suppose so," she said with a sigh. "If you want to. But don't you have to go to work?"

"I am early. There is still time. The iron in the ground will not run away."

They both laughed.

"No, I suppose not."

They walked along in silence. Indian summer was in full effect and the warm bright sunlight belied the coming winter chill with merely a promise of frost in the slight northern breeze. They passed the home of the 'Captain'—the mine superintendent, and Adele felt ashamed that Johnny would see the small miner's shack she lived in. Her family's home was dwarfed by the three-story mansion the Captain and his family lived in, with its huge front porch and gabled roof. But, of course Johnny's family lived in one of the shacks as well, so she knew she was worried heedlessly.

"Do you miss school?" Adele suddenly asked.

59

"Yes, a little," he replied. "I missed the fun and the playground. The English and Math lessons not so much."

She laughed.

"I do miss my friends," he said sadly, but straightened to his full height, "but now I am helping my family."

"My brother Ken starts there next week."

"Yes, I know. He will work with me."

"Will you—?"

"Of course, Kenver is my friend. I will watch out for him and teach him."

"Is it terribly dangerous?" She asked, but knew the truth already. She had grown to dread the three blasts of the mine whistle that signaled an emergency, and had attended several funerals of men killed in accidents. She had even heard the rumors of the field on the far end of town where it was said the bachelors who had no family to claim their bodies were buried by the mining company in shallow and unmarked graves.

They followed the path down the hollow until they reached her small wooden framed home where her mother was hanging some washing out back, while her younger sisters and brothers ran around the yard playing chase. She turned to face Johnny and stared into his friendly and handsome face.

"Will you be coming to the winter dance?" she asked. "My father will be playing his fiddle."

"Is it only for Cousin Jacks? Or will a poor Finn be allowed in?"

"It is for everyone. My father says we are all Americans now."

"Then I will be there," Johnny smiled kindly. "And I hope you will," he faltered and spoke quietly, "dance with me."

"We will see," she said coyly and suppressed her smile.

"Well, I had better go to the mine. They take an hour's pay away if you are a minute late," he said and turned to go.

"Goodbye Johnny," she replied sweetly and started to carry her basket inside.

Johnny suddenly stopped, turned around and came back to stand in front of her, his large frame towering over her.

"Miss Adele," he started.

"What is it, Johnny?"

"I think—"

"Don't just stand there with your mouth open, you look like a trout out of water," she said taunting him. He turned bright red.

"I think you are pretty," he blurted out and turned and ran as hard as he could toward the mine tower that stood in the distance.

It was Adele's turn to blush. Her thoughts were swept up by dreams of dancing with the tall Finnish boy; and she dearly wished the months would fly by and that soon a cascade of twinkling snowflakes would be falling all around her as he held her tightly in his strong arms.

CHAPTER FIFTEEN

"Come on, Betty," the young man with the stringy blonde hair and puppy dog eyes begged, while learning on the bar surrounded by a scruffy group of teenaged friends in the gloomy, dark environs of Crystal Falls' dingiest tavern, the Lakeside.

"No way, Jeremy," the older female bartender argued. While rough looking, with her matted hair, tobacco-stained teeth and a myriad of tattoos, she did exude a certain feminine charm as she leaned over the bar pretending to wipe up stains with a nasty cloth —giving the wide-eyed boys an unimpeded peek down the valley of her ample bosom.

"You fooled me before, but I know who you are now and I don't plan on losing my license over you and your no-good friends. I had no idea you were 15 and s'posed to be in school. What I should'a done is told your ol' man on ya – that's what I ought'a done."

"He ain't my father," the young man snarled. She ignored the interjection and continued to wipe the counter top and give the boys a hard time.

"Sittin' here drinkin' and lyin' to me all the time about bein' in the army. Ya' all ought'a be ashamed of yourselves."

The teens huddled together in a pack muttering to each other for moment before Jeremy shushed them and, turning back to her, addressed the woman behind the bar.

"Well if you won't let us drink here, sell us a 12-pack for the road at least."

"I can't do that."

"Oh come on sweetie," Jeremy sweetened the tone of his voice.

"Don'cha do it. Don'cha look at me with those blue eyes or I'll git the giggles. Oh hell alright, I never much cared for school myself. I don't see any harm in it. Just don't you dare tell your dad that I was the one that sold it to ya."

"He ain't my dad."

The boys dug in their pockets and handed the woman a handful of crumpled bills and spare change.

"What do you think this is the Salvation Army? Do I look like I'm ringing a bell? And you're two dollars and 17 cents short."

"Aw, give us a break—you're charging us double what we could get it for down at the Jubilee."

"Yeah, and you can just go on down there and show 'em your IDs while you're at it."

Jeremy leaned in close and whispered, "How about you give us some credit—you know I'm good for it. Maybe we could work out a trade?"

Betty blushed and giggled. "Might have to take you up on that one of these nights. But don't let Chester hear ya' – he's jealous as all get out and with a temper like you don't even know. Gave me a real nice shiner a few months back just for chatting a bit with the beer salesman. Well okay, the guy did kiss me... once... or well maybe a few times. He was cute and young. But Ches found out, guess maybe I let it slip, and he broke the guys arm next time he showed up with a delivery. The company had to send us a new fella, but he's ugly, married and a Christian to top it all off. Don't know why Chester can't see a girl has to have a little fun being stuck here with a bunch of drunks and you-know-whats, especially with him always off hunting, or whatever him and your dad and his pals are always up to."

Jeremy gritted his teeth and spit the words out, "Junior is not my dad. My dad ran off when I was just a kid."

"That, or someone killed him is more likely." Jeremy flinched and noticing his reaction, Betty softened her tone. "Guess I probably shouldn't a said that, but it's true. He was wilder than the wind and made himself quite a few enemies for sure, including your dad, I mean step-dad, er... Junior. They weren't exactly friendly and all, what with June bein' a cop and all and your daddy always bein' up to no good, dealing drugs and stuff. Whole town 'bout had a conniption when your mama took up with June after Jess done run out on her or got killed or whatever. No one could figure it out. Guess she wanted to give ya' a good home after all

63

she'd been through growin' up with that batty Jehovah's witness of a mom and ol' Red the dog poisoning pervert. You probably already know this but ya know her stepdad Red died right here in this bar. Heart attack—right where you're standing now. No, just kiddin' ya—he was in the can sitting on the shitter—can ya imagine that? What a way to go. He really went I tell ya."

The bartender brayed with laughter, as Jeremy listened sullenly.

"But yeah, your mom and Junior… some folks would'a laid money on him bein' gay or doin' the deed with his own mother. But don't tell him I said nothin,' I hear tell from Ches that June's got himself quite the temper and there's some bodies buried 'round here could probably attest to it if they could."

"Whatever," Jeremy muttered impatiently. "How about you throw in a bottle of the good stuff too, Bets?"

"I ain't giving you any good stuff, Jeremy. Ches would kill me. Here—you can have this bottle of Everclear, but you owe me."

"I'm good for it."

"You better be," she said in voice as smooth and sweet as syrup as she winked at the boy.

CHAPTER SIXTEEN

"June, can I see you for a moment?"

The creaky voice erupting from the interior of the office across the room crashed like a wave breaking against the rocky shore of his solitude causing Junior's heart to plummet.

"Sure Sid," he called out without enthusiasm, adding, "Not like I got anything better to do," under his breath.

Sliding the paperwork on his desk quickly into neat piles, the heavy-set officer wheeled his chair back, rose from his seat, and lumbered smoothly into the recesses of the Sheriff's office where only through his exceptionally quick reaction time did he miss getting hit in the eye with a fishing fly.

"Whoops, sorry about that, June," the grizzled, gray-haired man behind the desk across the office wearing a fishing hat, vest and waders giggled as he yanked and swished his rod. "Wasn't expecting you to be so damn quick on the draw. How do you like the new outfit? An anniversary present from the wife—gonna try it out tonight after the meeting."

Big Sid was the Sheriff and had been ever since Junior's father had died suddenly, legendarily in the throes of illicit love, a few years back. Sid had been Roy Senior's right hand man and was known less for being a tough guy than for his ability to stay calm and to smooth situations over, usually when the Sheriff's temper got the better of him beating a transient or working girl a little too hard, as he was wont to do. In fact, it was hard to imagine a less fearsome character inhabiting an office that seemed to often require a harsh and inordinate expression of power and the omnipresent threat of violence. But the locals, perhaps fearing the return of Roy Sr.'s ghost—many did not believe he had died even after the open-casket viewing and funeral—and knowing Sid still did command a group of ferocious goons, continued to pay up the bribes, protection monies and shares from the ongoing gambling, prostitution and drugs endeavors.

As a Senior Leader of the Junior Pioneers youth group, Sid had learned advanced survival skills and he had a mean streak that belied his placid and innocuous appearance and, as such, he kept things running as smoothly as they always had for years. Perhaps the most bizarre aspect to this story was that Big Sid wasn't all that big—just kind of average-sized to be honest. Junior never knew or cared to know where he got the nickname.

"What's this all about? Did I do anything wrong… again?" Junior asked, barely concealing his irritation.

"Oh hell no, nothing like that," the Sheriff replied distractedly while he worked on achieving just the right wrist angle, and nearly hooking the fly on the stuffed moose head hanging on the wall behind him in the process. "No, no, we're all real happy with your work, June. You're a chip off the old man's block and, if you keep up the continued effort and enthusiasm, I believe we will see you sitting in this here chair someday and making the old boy proud as punch."

"Gonna be a few years yet, Sid, I'm sure," Junior said assuming his smoothest tone of voice. "I mean, you aren't ready to retire yet, right? Or are you?"

"Oh ho. Not a chance. The wife would like it for sure, don'tcha know, but I figure I got a few years left and gotta sock away some more candy for the retirement years, if you know what I mean."

"Sure boss. I get your point. I got a sweet tooth myself."

"A sweet tooth!" The man's eyes bulged. "Oh June that's a good one. You crack me right up but good. Anybody ever tell you you're a funny guy?" He tightened the slack on the line and snickered as he made the fly jump across the carpet. "Now you don't worry, I'll work you into the 'candy store biz' nice and slow. Wouldn't want to give ya' a diabetic coma by eating too much 'sugar' right away, eh?"

"I don't know. I'm pretty sure I can handle it. I can taste it already."

"Um hmmm sweet as a big ol' chocolate bar too. Hershey's milk chocolate of course. We don't go for any of that fruity French or Swiss stuff 'round here. No sir, we like it made right here in the good ol' USA. But you got plenty of time for that, June. It's like they say in the good book—'patience is a virtue,' you know."

The hook suddenly caught and became tangled in the carpet. Sid frowned and struggled for a moment to dislodge it as Junior watched on in embarrassed dismay. Finally, the deputy bent over and reached down with a pudgy hand and unhooked the fly before straightening himself up and continuing.

"Yeah right. 'Patience.' So what is it you wanted to see me about, Sid?"

Forced to return his focus to business, the Sheriff sighed and sat down behind his desk, motioning Junior to take a seat in one of the uncomfortable chairs across the desk from him.

"Well hell, I know you've seen all this hullabaloo about them missing kids and all—they got them damn flyers hanging on every shop window and on all the light poles around here too."

Junior felt his body tense.

"Yeah, what about them?" he asked with feigned nonchalance.

"It turns out one of the kid's father is that rich bastard, Lance Taylor who owns all those corporations and hotels and golf courses and stuff and he's raising all sorts of stink about it and throwin' his weight around like those rich dudes tend to do when they get upset. Giving me all sorts of grief just because the kids came through Crystal Falls and now they can't find them."

"That so?" the deputy muttered tersely.

"Aw, it's probably just a bunch of nonsense and they're doped up on drugs somewhere, or who knows maybe they went and made a fuss on the 'Res.' They stole some beer from here in town you know. That kind of behavior by some spoiled white brats ain't gonna fly over in Chippewa territory. They coulda' got themselves scalped and then... well, good luck finding their hides out there in 'wagon burner' territory."

"Yeah so some rich punks drove through town, so what? What are we supposed to do about it? We looked for them already. They aren't here."

"Well now, that's what I've been saying, but this Taylor guy is dead set on making some big waves about it. I tried to shut him up and told him to just let us do our job, but he just keeps calling and shouting he's gonna call in the FBI and the National Guard and all."

Junior's attention was drawn away by the portrait hanging on the wall to the left of his boss of George W. Bush—smiling broadly for the camera as he shook Sid's hand.

"And anyway, like I was sayin' before," the Sheriff continued in his homespun drone, "you were on duty that day, and there's always a chance they might have gone south out of town you know —out where you were…patrolling."

Junior shifted his vision to the calendar on the wall to the Sheriff's right. A lovely forest scene with a waterfall pouring itself into a deep and placid blue pond. He looked away quickly.

"Apparently they were speeding through town in a bright red Camaro—can't miss that—and I know you said you didn't see anything, but… are you sure you didn't see nothin' of them boys?"

Junior took a deep breath and thought about his father. How would his father have handled this? His face reddened and he blurted out his response in a wave of anger.

"Dammit Sid, if I would've seen them don't you think I'd be the first one to say something—"

The Sheriff shook his head in agreement and fondled his rod lovingly as Junior continued.

"—hell, maybe this Taylor guy would be more 'appreciative' of my abilities than the local authorities seem to be, and just maybe he gives me a big reward. Or maybe he's so impressed with my information he decides he needs a new chief of security for that mansion of his out on that fancy island he owns."

The Sheriff held up his hand to quiet Junior's rising voice.

"Yeah, yeah, I know, June. Don't get your panties in a bunch. Those boys probably went out of town north and slipped on up over to the Porkies and got themselves lost is all. But I figured I better cover all the bases before the rich asshole shows up on our doorstep."

"He isn't coming here is he?" Junior hissed.

"Sure is. He'll be here in a couple days. Bringing a whole posse with him too. We'd better be careful or there'll be a hangin' vigilante style. You ok June,? You look a little pale."

"I'm good. Just hungry. Think I just need a candy bar."

"Oh ho ho. Damn, you sure got your Daddy's sense of humor didn't you?"

"I don't remember my father ever smiling, let alone laughing," Junior replied sullenly.

"Oh, your Daddy was a hoot. I got stories I could tell, but hell, this ain't the time or place. You and the missus still comin' over for dinner tomorrow night, right? Nancy's got a new venison pot roast recipe she's been dying to try out on somebody for ages."

"I'll be there for sure. Jen's been sick lately, so not sure about her."

"Heck June, that girl of yours is sure sick all the time. Darn it, Nancy's gonna get all offended and think she's avoiding us if she don't make it this time."

"Yeah she is pretty sickly. I'll see what I can do. You know how women are."

"You got that right, June," Sid said vacantly, itching to get back to his casting. "Will you close the door on your way out? I got some… reports to go over."

Junior closed the door on his way out with a slam.

CHAPTER SEVENTEEN

Eidolon!

Why must you torment me? Just when I think you have finally faded away you return like the recurring curtain of mist draped over the Paint River nearly every morning.

And stare at me with angry, accusing eyes.

I close my eyes and still I see you.

You are dead, I know. I know it well. I killed you, didn't I? Yet you stand there, silent and hard and unforgiving.

Your face still shining, Jesse, haloed by your long blonde hair and unshaven cheeks and flashing eyes and mocking grin, though I know that your flesh has rotted away and melted from your bones in your lonely grave on the island in the Michigamme Reservoir years ago.

What I have done is unforgivable, but you must have mercy in you. I have been punished enough by my own guilt, ever since I cracked your skull with a rock and felt your warm blood cover my hands as you breathed out your final choking bit of life.

I knelt and washed your blood and dirt from your grave off my hands in the cold waters… and yet it has never been washed clean, not ever.

And what was it for? What was it all for after all?

Everything I did was for Jenny. No, I lie, it was for myself.

But in the end, it was for nothing.

Nothing.

I lie here night after night trapped in my broken body and sometimes you come to me again, like you used to when we were children and you were frightened because that crazy son-of-a bitch father of yours was drunk and in a vile temper. I used to comfort you. I gave you companionship and a peaceful respite to escape to from the whirlwind of your tormented life. Can't you remember that?

Now you come to see me only to watch me suffer.

And smile at my pain.

Dissipate apparition. Merge back into the shadows from which you came. Drift away, silently, harmlessly, into the aether, like the fine-filigreed tracery of smoke of a dying candle flame—one snuffed out in an act of violence, just as I once, engulfed in the agonies of jealousy, extinguished your bright young light here on earth and now must endure this interminable, torturous and tormented twilight.

I beg you to forgive me.

Forgive me.

Eidolon.

CHAPTER EIGHTEEN

The room in the basement of the church had dim lighting and a low, yellow-stained ceiling, that seemed to trap the air within its tight enclosure. Upon descending the creaking steps and entering the room, a visitor finds themselves submerged into a musty, pungent atmosphere smelling of old rugs desperately needing replacement unpleasantly mixing with the bitter aroma of cheap coffee percolating in the stainless steel clad kitchen at the back of the room. Ammonia and cheap dish detergent flavors mingle with the smell of chalk from the children's classroom down the cracked linoleum hallway adding to the blend of seasoning to the redolence.

Memories of meetings and gatherings have been preserved in the atmosphere of the room. Bible study groups with prayers and gossip, sat in uncomfortable folding chairs, spilling coffee and cookie crumbs on the carpeting, and staining the off-white tablecloths that draped the asymmetrical configuration of round and rectangular tables as they sought communion with each other and their God. The local Cub Scouts dripped paint and glue onto the floor and ground crayon goo of red and blue into the golden fibers as they ran chasing one another, oblivious to the sacred and serious nature of the building above. The Red Cross nobly utilized the room for its quarterly blood drive, while the alcoholic 'sinners' in A.A. shared their stammering, guilt-ridden confessions and sorrows every Tuesday.

For a time, a mixed choir practiced here; a shaggy-haired youth group played acoustic guitars and sang folk songs here in the '60s; while a barbershop quartet's voices reverberated off the walls prior to that. In much earlier times, a temperance society held fiery meetings here; more recently the Girl Scouts giggled and practiced knots. It was even rumored that a former pastor held private sessions with a young parishioner in the darkness of this room, but that was many years ago and never spoken of these days.

Throughout the passing years—indeed decades, the individuals who had sojourned here left an imprint upon the room; and the ancient echoes of their thoughts and voices continued to linger in the air, filling it with a weighty sense of time that emanated gloomily from the heavy dark wood-paneled walls and velvet draperies.

On this particular evening, as the handful of people surrounding her milled about, a tall woman dominated the center of the room—appearing from a distance to resemble a large flowering shrub in full bloom. Her printed smock exhibited a garish multi-colored floral design matching her wide-brimmed hat, while her curly grey hair protruded in tufts of bushy billows above a bulbous and fleshy face. The thickness of her mannish legs— prominently displayed below her short shift, resembled the sturdy trunks of a rugged oak tree; while her rather massive bulk and wide shoulders would be the envy of many a defensive lineman. She towered over the other attendees, including the aged Pastor Carlsson, who quaked and cowered as she barked orders in a loud masculine voice in his direction.

"Move that over here, Pastor," she demanded, pointing to a table. "And please make it quick" The woman spoke loudly, often clapping her hands together to emphasize her commands. "People are arriving and we need to get things moving along promptly. As I told you before, I cannot be here all night as I have important letters to write to some of our elected officials. Therefore, we must be quite sure that we have clearly communicated our expectations in advance to the participants in order to obtain strict adherence to the rules of order, thus ensuring that a successful and productive meeting ensues."

The bony pastor bent his crooked back over the table and cringed in pain as he attempted to pull it across the carpet to the appointed spot.

"Ms. Hurlburt" he said, huffing from the exertion, "this is intended merely as an informal gathering to discuss—"

"Nonsense, Pastor," the resounding voice rang out with authority, "we must have order. Without order we would simply have... disorder." She waved her lanky arms about as if she were the Queen of Hearts surveying her army of playing cards.

"Am I right, Sue Lee?" she continued, orbiting her bulky mass, as if on a swivel, to address a mousy Oriental woman, who jumped visibly at the attention.

"I... I...believe so, Ms. Hurl—"

"You see Pastor, Sue Lee agrees with me, and I'm sure if we ask the others, they would understand the need for this meeting to aspire to the glory of classical Greek *demokratia* and not simply digress to the level of a drunken shouting match." She squinted suspiciously at a rather shabbily-dressed, long-haired man busily stuffing cookies into his mouth and pockets. "Unless you would prefer to move this gathering to the Lakeside, Pastor?"

"Of course not," the old man replied with a shudder at the thought of normal people trapped within the notorious drinking hole that was considered by right-thinking citizens to be a virtual mouth to hell for the riots, rapes and murders, real or imagined, that had occurred over the years.

"I should think not," the matron sputtered, before glaring and shouting at the greedy gobbler, "You there!" Stomping across the floor she accosted the startled fellow, who dropped a handful of cookies onto the floor and retreated quickly into the mens' room, with the bellowing behemoth following in pursuit, her voice echoing off the tiles.

An older man and woman sullenly entered the room wearing raincoats and carrying umbrellas. "Hello Art, Hello Janice," Pastor Carlsson said greeting the duo. "I didn't know there was rain expected tonight."

"There isn't," snapped the man with evident ill-temper, while his wife just looked at the ground goggle-eyed. They both turned away to hang up their rain gear, ignoring the pastor's outstretched hand offered in greeting.

Treading softly, a short man wearing thick glasses entered and took a seat at the back of the room facing away from the group.

"Benny," Pastor Carlsson called out in friendly voice, "we are all sitting over here. Please come and join us." He gestured to the table he had just finished moving.

"I'm good here, Pastor," the man said and faced away. Before the pastor could respond, he was unexpectedly accosted by a pair of elderly twin sisters who had gingerly descended the uneven stairs clutching each other's arms.

"Hello Pastor," the slightly taller one squeaked.

"Yes, Hello Pastor," he sister parroted.

"Bronnen, Beryan, how nice to see you—"

"Before the meeting begins," the taller sister interrupted, "we must ask."

"Yes, we must ask."

"Do you have Decaf?"

"We must have Decaf," the other chimed in.

"You see, our doctor—"

"Our doctor says—"

"She says—"

"She says we must—"

"Yes, we must—"

"That is what she says—"

"She is a lady doctor—"

"A lady yes—"

"And a doctor—"

"Yes—"

"Anyway—"

"Yes—"

"Decaf?"

"Yes, decaf. Decaffeinated coffee."

"Do you have it?"

"Do you?"

"I believe we have both regular coffee as well as decaffeinated in the kitchen," the pastor replied when he could finally get a word in, and without any delay, the two women proceeded arm in arm across the floor toward the kitchen.

Timing his entrance with precision, another elderly man, dressed in a worn-out, tan sport coat and jeans, sidled up to the pastor, managing to avoid the ladies' attention as they left on their search for their doctor-prescribed drink of choice.

"Well, well, the Ferris sisters showed up? Did they bring their ventriloquist with them?"

"Now Stan, please try to be civil."

"Alright, alright, I'll make nice. I'd be best buds with Satan himself to get that fat ass Junior run out of town."

"That's odd Stan, I always thought you were good friends with Sheriff Pultz?"

"Junior has no friends, only victims."

"Stanley!"

77

"You have to make nice with him, you know that Pastor. But I'd love to see him get his. That protection money I pay him is killing me, I might have to close up the hardware store."

"Well, I am hopeful that you have had a change of heart and are willing to help lead our crusade then,"

"Are you kidding? I snuck in here the back way and I'll be gone as soon as I can, before anybody knows I'm here. Junior would kill me quick if he knew I was here."

"How can we be sure you aren't here spying on us and are planning to run back to the Sheriff and let him know our plans?" Pastor Carlsson inquired.

"Pastor, you know me. Does that sound like something I would do?"

"Hmmm," the Pastor stared hard into Stan's eyes until the man looked away nervously.

"So where is the 'Man of the Hour' anyway?" he asked.

"I told Ethan to stop by a little later, after we take the temperature of the crowd."

"Of these stiffs? Don't get me wrong, I want Junior gone as much as anyone, but this little team of yours couldn't beat a team of schoolgirls, let alone a ruthless S.O.B. like Junior."

"You have to start somewhere, Stan. Look at Jesus, Gandhi—"

"Tom Duncan?"

"Who?"

"That drifter kid who got drunk and tried to rob Dilly's gas station."

"Yeah, I remember him; Junior and his boys took him out of town and sent him on his way."

"You mean took him on a one-way trip out of town and straight to Hades."

"You mean—" the pastor stammered.

"The way I hear it, things got a little out of hand while teaching the suspect a lesson. He got a nice resting place out in the swamp they say."

"Oh no. No…." The pastor shook his head. "But he was just a stupid kid. Stupid is all. There wasn't any reason… Damn it—"

"Careful Padre, you know things are serious when you start cursing."

"I apologize, it's just…"

"I know, I know, but are you sure you want to go up against that bastard and his crew with this lame ass bunch of clowns?" Stan sipped his coffee as the pastor silently surveying the small group gathered in the basement.

"Attention everyone!" the brassy voice suddenly boomed across the room, causing Stan to spill his coffee down the front of his shirt. "Everyone take a seat here at once so we can begin!"

The assembled group gathered together around the table. "That means you too, young man," she said with authority to Benny, who arose timidly and reluctantly joined the group.

"Now before the meeting begins, I must make everyone familiar with the rules."

"Ms. Hurlburt, I hardly think such protocol to be necessary—"

"I disagree Pastor, I believe it to be most necessary to maintaining an orderly and civil meeting. Now then please listen closely as I will be very clear and do not feel I should need to repeat any of these instructions once I have finished."

Pastor Carlsson rolled his eyes as the verbal onslaught began.

"We will be following the rules of parliamentary procedure. Firstly, you may obtain the floor by being the first to stand when the person speaking has finished. You must address me as Madam Chairman and must be recognized by the Chair before speaking. Do not raise your hand as this action means nothing, and do not stand up while another has the floor or you will be ruled out of order!"

The seedy-looking young man who had been accosted earlier in the restroom and was now seated uncomfortably across from the chairwoman raised his hand. Ms. Hurlburt sighed.

"What is it?"

"Did you say, not to raise our hands, or we can raise our hands but only if it's important?"

"Did I, or did I not say, you are not to hold up your hand?" she appealed to the attendees.

Some mumbled yes, some shook their heads, Janice stared at the table and grinned.

"You are not to raise your hand," Ms. Hurlburt stated solemnly. "Now then, debate will not begin until the Chair has stated the motion or resolution and asked 'are you ready for the question?' If no one rises, the chair will call for the vote!"

The young man raised his hand, a look of confusion on his face.

"What did I say?" Ms. Hurlburt snarled. He lowered his hand and she continued.

"Where were we? Oh yes, Before the motion is stated by the Chair, members may suggest modification of the motion—"

"Oh oh oh!" The young man raised his hand again. I know what I wanted to ask."

"And what, pray tell, is that?" Ms. Hurlburt asked with exasperation.

"What if we have to go to the bathroom?"

"Hold it!" she shouted. The young man sank back into his seat.

"Now then, the mover can modify as he pleases, or even withdraw the motion without consent of the seconder; if the mover choses to modifies, the seconder can withdraw the second—"

"Point of Parliamentary Procedure!" Stan Jacobsen interjected with exasperation.

"Stanley, we have not even begun the meeting, you don't need to—"

"Well, I have a question about something and you said we aren't allowed to raise our hands, so how the hell else do I get you quit talking?"

"I beg your pardon?"

"I mean why can't we just get on to the real reason we are all here? As in electing a new Sheriff and getting rid of that A-hole, Junior and his corrupt bunch of cronies for good."

"You know perfectly well, that before we get to new business we must first read and approve the minutes. There is a procedure that must be followed. We must hear the reports of the officers, boards and standing committees, the reports of the special committees, any special orders, unfinished business and general orders—"

"This is our first meeting—there are no minutes to read, or committees to report, standing or otherwise, you wacky old bat!" Stan shouted.

"You are out of order," Ms. Hurlburt snapped, her face reddening to crimson. "Remarks must be courteous in language and deportment!"

"How can I be out of order, when the meeting hasn't even started?"

At this point Benny stood up, his face white, and visibly shaking started walking toward the door, muttering under his breath, "Not the Sheriff, not Junior, no I won't do that. He might hit me again."

"Get back here and quit mumbling, you lousy coward," Art erupted suddenly, but the frightened man hurriedly gathered his coat and disappeared out the door.

Art stared after him and shouted angrily. "Junior killed my son. Don't you care? Doesn't anyone care? Look what he did to her. Look what he did to my wife."

Janice looked at the table and smiled at her cookie.

"Aw, you don't care. None of you. Nobody cares." The angry man sat down, suppressing a sob as he did.

A silence fell over the group, but before Pastor Carlsson could clear his throat and, the group was distracted by the entrance of a heavy set young woman wearing a waitress uniform, who noisily emerged into the room carrying an infant and dragging two shrieking young children, a boy and a girl behind her.

"Sorry about this everyone," the woman apologized, "but my babysitter bailed. Ran off with their father if you must know, so hope you don't mind that I brung the brats along. Now you two just shut up and be quiet!" She slapped both the toddlers in the face, the punishment simply causing them to wail louder, which, in turn, started the baby crying as well.

"Point of Privilege!" shouted one twin.

"Point of Privilege!" shouted the other.

"I move we ban loud screaming children from this important political meeting," Ms. Hurlburt pronounced.

"I second the motion," muttered Stan.

The young man's face registered an even greater degree of confusion and he meekly raised his hand again.

"What is it now?" hissed Ms. Hurlburt.

"I thought... I mean... isn't this the A.A. meeting?"

At this point, a well-dressed, muscular man entered the room and the pandemonium immediately ceased. Even the children stopped their crying and stared with wide eyes as the tall and noble figure of a smiling, confident man strode purposely to the head of the table where he addressed the attendees smoothly in a deep and strong voice.

"Hello everyone. I want to thank you for coming tonight. My name is Ethan Anderson and with the help from loyal citizens such as yourselves, I am going to be the next sheriff here in Iron County."

CHAPTER NINETEEN

Startled at the sudden sound, the man awoke. He listened intently for a moment and then reached over and fumbled for his glasses on the bed stand. He couldn't be sure, but it sure sounded like something was in his house.

In the kitchen? He thought he heard the thump of soft footsteps padding across the linoleum floor. Maneuvering his stiff body upright with the usual difficulty, he put his glasses in place on his large nose and—heart thumping hard, listened carefully for the sound of movement in the blackness.

Frankly, he was surprised he'd heard anything at all; he was half deaf and his wife used to say he'd sleep through both Armageddon and the Rapture itself—snoring away while the dead were rising and heavenly angels sang the Hallelujah Chorus. Of course she was long dead now, and even though she was a terrible nag, who nearly drove him to kill himself via the slow, sad death by poison (as in cheap whiskey and beer), there were times he did miss feeling the warmth of her body next to him in bed.

There it was again. He wasn't dreaming after all. Just a small creak in the floor. He knew this house and all of its squeaks and moans as well as he knew his own body. That one was a familiar floorboard that he always thought sounded like he imagined a mast on a schooner about to break in a gale sounded. Not that he had ever been on ship in his life, but he'd seen some pirate movies and had just always associated it with that kind of a sound. But that floorboard wouldn't play its refrain without some sort of pressure, and he was alone in his house now. The realization of this fact caused his eyes to focus and his mind to become fully alert.

As he gathered his wits, he wished he still had Daisy. Not his wife, no, Daisy was his beagle. She was a good girl. But he had to put her down a couple years back and never replaced her. He had

had enough of death and just didn't want to ever go through that again. His wife dying was bad enough, but to hold that poor whimpering pup as they injected her she went limp...

A skittering sound. It was probably a coon. He relaxed. Yes, he must have left the back door ajar and the pest must have gotten in to get at the garbage. He smiled when he thought how his girl— Daisy that is, would have taken care of the intruder; she wasn't real brave, but she could carry on barking and howling like you wouldn't believe.

But hell, he was glad he didn't have the damn dog anymore. Too much trouble. And now he could go wherever he wanted whenever he felt like it. Of course, you had to have somewhere to go, or even somewhere you wanted to go and he just... didn't. He didn't even remember the last time he left the house. All his friends, if you could call them that, were mostly dead or moved on down south somewhere. He should do that. Maybe find himself a rich widow to look after him. But he knew he never would. He knew the ladies were probably desperate for companionship, but... he had no money, very little hair and looked like a walking skeleton these days. And what with the drinking problem, the shakes and the prostrate that was acting funny, well... might as well just hang in here and wait for the reaper and take his medicine when it comes.

A loud clink from the kitchen. What the hell? He stepped off the bed, slid his feet into his slippers and stumbled quietly across the room and down the hallway. *Damn coon. Might have to use a broom and chase him out. Gotta be careful though—those things can have rabies and they will bite you good if you get them cornered.*

As he approached the kitchen, he heard something else and felt a chill. *Was that...? Yes it was—water running. A coon wouldn't do that.*

He flipped on the light and entered the room.

The boy at the table was drinking a glass of water and eating a sandwich. He looked up at the man and wearily began to raise his gun.

The old man froze in shock—and then felt a sudden sharp pain in his chest. Gasping, he clutched at his throat as he struggled to breath—his eyes bulging as he collapsed choking and convulsing to the floor.

The boy, carrying his rifle, glass of water and a sandwich on a plate, stepped carefully around the man whose contorted body shook and writhed in pain on the linoleum—arms extended like a drowning man desperately seeking a life preserver in a stormy sea.

Shrugging and thinking to himself, *Hey, I saved a bullet for the next one*, the boy sat down on the lumpy couch in the living room, turned on the TV and adjusted the volume. The exaggerated Boings, Zips and Whizzes emitted during the cartoon cats and mice violent, yet comic battles, soon covered up the garbled cries coming from twisted mouth until finally the last tortured breaths died painfully away.

The sandwich tasted good, the boy thought as he curled up and fell asleep holding his rifle tight in his arms.

CHAPTER TWENTY

The intense man stood at the front of the room and faced the restless group of deputies gathered in the room—his graying hair sleekly jelled back, his expensive suit impeccable. He spoke in masterful voice, as if he were comfortable speaking to large groups on a regular basis and impressed everyone with his smooth, yet aggressive manner. His stern, intelligent eyes focused on the gathered individuals as he addressed them with an accent that only slightly betrayed his Jersey upbringing. From his body language and the way he aggressively punctuated his speech with his hands when he spoke, it was clear that he was used to being the alpha dog in any situation.

"I assume that you all know who I am and why I'm here, but just in case you aren't aware, my name is Lance Taylor and this is my ex-wife, Sharon—who I'm sure you already know owns the flower shop over in Iron Mountain."

He put an arm around the shoulders of a statuesque, middle-aged blonde with an excessively fake tanned face, whose wrinkled face and red eyes revealed the telltale signs of several days' worth of tears.

"As many of you may know," the speaker continued. "I own several companies that some of you may have heard of, including Taylor Tractors and Monolith Insurers and I am one of the biggest employers in the state. And I... we are here visiting you today because we want to ask you all for your assistance in helping us find our son Cole and his friend Jim Denton. Now as you know, the boys were last seen in Crystal Falls, where they engaged in some unfortunate adolescent mischief—"

"Like shoplifting some beer at the gas station," Deputy Torvalds whispered to Junior in the back of the room where they were seated."

"—which was caught on the surveillance camera at the gas station. That was, unfortunately, the last time they were seen."

The man paused to let his point sink in. The men in the room shifted uncomfortably in their chairs as Taylor paused and stared at them for a beat before recommencing his lecture.

"We are unsure as to what direction the boys may have gone upon leaving Crystal Falls—"

"Escaping is more like it," Torvalds hissed.

"—and as you all are certainly aware, there are many back roads around here which the boys may have taken. I understand from the Sheriff here that the woods are deep and thick enough that the boys may have gotten disoriented and abandoned their vehicle after perhaps running out of gas or God forbid, having an accident. We believe they may have carried fishing gear, sleeping bags, tents and other camping paraphernalia, so it is possible that they have just decided to play a prank on us all, similar to Tom and Huck in that famous Mark Twain story—"

"What is he talking about?"

"It's a book, dummy," Junior snapped.

"—and they are just out camping somewhere and rather self-centeredly refusing to make contact with their families. Or maybe they decided to rebel and take off and join the circus or make a new life somewhere. I would understand. I left home when I was 15 to escape an abusive stepfather and make my way in the world myself. Didn't work out so bad for me."

"You think?"

"Shut up Torvalds."

"Maybe they took off for California, maybe Canada, or maybe they turned around and snuck back home and are partying right now in Grosse Point right under our noses. Or, and here's another idea, maybe they went out searching for some of that buried treasure you're so famous for and... they are lost or trapped in one of the abandoned mines somewhere in this area."

Muffled muttering filled the room. Sharon sobbed. Taylor wiped his forehead with a silk handkerchief and softened his tone.

"In any case, Sharon and I implore you to help us. I know some of you here are parents of your own. I... we lost our oldest son to a boating accident five years ago and Cole is all we have left."

Carefully folding and replacing the handkerchief back into his breast pocket, Taylor paced the floor in a manner that suggested at untold reserves of energy vibrating just beneath the surface.

"I can assure you all that these truly are good boys, despite their reckless nature and unfortunate disrespect for the law, for which I can assure you they will be punished."

"What, take away their allowance for a day?"

"Dammit Torvalds."

Taylor stopped speaking and glared long at Junior, his eyes searching the expression on the deputy's face for several long seconds. Junior felt a drop of sweat run down his brow but stared back at his inquisitor emotionlessly until Taylor started up again.

"Now, we were under the impression the boys were planning to go the Porcupine Mountains," Taylor continued. "at least that is the story they told a few friends, and we have been in contact with the Tribal Police on the reservation, but as you know, they are... their own nation and have been... less than assiduous in providing assistance."

"Acid what?"

"They maintain that to their knowledge, no one in the tribe has seen the boys. Our biggest fear is that the young men's somewhat naïveté—"

"Speak English or go home."

"Shhhhh"

"—may have led them to possibly have been taken advantage of by... undesirable elements. They were driving a rather expensive new sports car—Cole's birthday present, and had a number of items—watches for example, that may have led them to attract the attention of criminals. While we pray the boys did not meet with foul play, we are convinced that time is of the essence, and as such am offering a substantial reward for the return of these children."

Sharon sobbed loudly. Lance squeezed her tightly across her shoulders.

"Now I have also enlisted the expertise of two private detectives—Mr. Powell and Mr. Wheeler, who are both here with us today, and who will be conducting their own investigation into this matter—"

"What the fuck?"

Taylor motioned to two large and serious looking men, who entered the room and stood behind him—one white, presumably Powell, and one black who nodded when the name Wheeler was mentioned. Tall and strong, both men displayed chiseled physiques and their attentive, upright demeanor indicated a background that likely included years of military training. The outlined bulges under their suits advertised that they were armed; while the impassive look in their eyes indicated they would have no problem using their weaponry upon the slightest provocation.

"I hope your department and the local police will both give these men, myself and Sharon your full cooperation at all times as we seek to bring the boys home safely. Thank you Sheriff."

At this, Sid walked up and shaking Taylor's hand, addressed his staff.

"Mr. Taylor, I can assure you that my men and I will endeavor to do whatever it takes to find those boys of yours. Won't we fellas?

A slight mutter of agreement rose from the gathering.

Junior smiled a sad, sickly smile while silently screaming under his skin.

CHAPTER TWENTY-ONE

Jeremy and the other boys joked and jostled each other as they walked out of the back door of the Lakeside en masse, carrying the 12-pack of beer and bottle of Everclear, just in time to see Chester's pickup truck pull up on big tires with a lurch, gravel and dust spewing everywhere.

"Uh oh," Travis said, and without hesitation, he and Ryan ran into the woods.

Chester's bearded face glowed a deep red and his huge body was tensed for action as he climbed out of the truck and advanced rapidly with long strides toward Jeremy, his eyes wild with rage.

"What the hell do you think you're doing, punk?" he snarled as he approached.

"What's it to you?" Jeremy retorted.

"Did you get that beer from my bar? Did that stupid cunt give that to you?" He yelled loud enough for his wife inside to hear.

"She didn't give us the beer," said Jeremy hiding the bottle of Everclear inside his jacket. "We paid for it."

"What the fuck? Does she want us to lose our license?" He grabbed the 12 pack out of Speedy's hands.

"Hey, give that back," the kid whined.

"Yeah, we paid for that," Kyle ventured bravely.

"Fuck off! You ain't getting any beer from my bar."

"Hey, Betty sold it to us fair and square." Jeremy said, glaring at Chester.

"Yeah, Chester. Don't be a prick—"

The large man's heavy hand stuck out instantaneously, slapping Kyle flat to the ground, where he lay with tears in his eyes and wiping blood from his mouth. Speedy and Brendon backed away wide-eyed.

"Anybody else want to be next?" he roared, and started toward the back entrance.

"At least give us our money back," Jeremy stepped between Chester and the door.

"What money? I never saw any money. What are you little pricks gonna do, call the cops or something?" He laughed and tried to step around Jeremy, who moved into his path.

"Don't be an asshole. Give it back," Jeremy said with as much bravery as he could muster.

"Let it go, Jeremy," Speedy said nervously.

"Better listen to your friend and run along, kid," Chester said and again tried to walk around Jeremy. The boy puffed himself up as big as he could, but still only came up to the giant's shoulders.

"Oh a tough guy, huh?"

"Give us the beer or give us our money back," Jeremy said in a quavering voice.

"You want the beer?" Chester threw the 12-pack against the wall, splattering the cans into a mess of smashed cans and foamy liquid. "There you go, lick it up boys. Be my guest. And guess what cheating whore of a wife is gonna clean up this mess," he bellowed toward the bar door.

"I guess we'll let you have the beer. Just give us the money back and we'll be outta here," Jeremy stood his ground.

"Oh now, you want money, huh? Well I got twenty-five dollars in my wallet if you want to try and get it." He turned to Speedy and then to Kyle, who had climbed to his feet and was staring with hate filled eyes at the man. "Any takers? Well then how about we start with the little rat who has been sticking his dick in my fucking woman—"

Whirling in a sudden burst of rage, and in one aggressive motion, the rugged man took hold of a handful of Jeremy's long blond hair and yanked his head down hard—directly into the toe of his logging boot as he kicked it violently upward. Jeremy's world turned to red and the audible crack of his nose breaking caused the other two boys to sprint away, Chester shouting after them as they fled: "What's a matter pussies, don't you want your money?" The lights went out for Jeremy as his limp body fell hard to the ground.

"You better keep on running until you get home or I am going to track you down give you the same treatment I gave your friend here!"

Laughing hysterically, the man screamed toward the bar: "Hey Betty, you fucking stupid whore, why don't you come on out, your lover boy is waiting for ya."

A few short seconds later, Jeremy came to lying on the parking lot surface with dirt and blood smeared across his face. He could hear Chester's voice shouting across a great distance, even though the blurred image of the large man stood just above him, arms waving angrily. Jeremy reached his numb fingers out, grasping for anything—a rock or stick that he could use as a weapon, but his hands could only feel loose gravel on pavement.

"What the hell are you going on about now, Chester?" Jeremy could hear Betty's voice far away.

"No, don't come out," he mouthed, but could not make a sound.

"You want to fuck this little piece of shit?" Chester yelled. "I can't trust you to keep your panties on for one second when I'm not looking, can I? And now you're robbing the goddamn cradle too!"

Chester reared back and Jeremy felt an explosion of pain with the impact of another steel toe boot to his side and he cried out as several ribs snapped.

"You make me fucking sick," the giant screamed. "So I guess maybe I gotta teach you another lesson, you fucking whore. And it's gonna be one you'll remember, I'll tell you that, you bitch! But first, let me put this stinking little cockroach you are in love with out of his misery. Goodnight kid!"

He raised his foot aiming to stomp it directly on Jeremy's head, but the red and black haze had begun to clear from Jeremy's vision and the boy suddenly lurched his body to one side and rolled away.

The large man stomped his foot downward but missed the moving target and lost his balance. Surprised, Chester cried out, "Uhhhhh" and staggered, nearly falling to the ground.

Bounding up instantly but unsteadily to his feet, the boy stumbled forward on shaking legs and, reaching into his jacket, removed the bottle of Everclear and swung it with both hands using all the force he could put forth—smashing it into the side of the startled man's head as both the man and the teen plummeted into darkness and fell headlong onto the hard concrete surface of the Lakeside parking lot.

CHAPTER TWENTY-TWO

He rolled over, away from the moist warmth of her soft body, and faced the wall before speaking quietly, "You know this is a bad idea."

"Why is that?" she asked softly and shifted her body toward him, putting her arm around him and kissing his shoulder.

"Because I'll be leaving here just as soon as my mom is safe."

"Oh," she said dumbly.

As they lay together in silence, he scanned the old furniture and rows of framed photographs on Katy's bedroom wall and felt the sadness within him swell. Black and white images of loving couples from the past looked down at him from beyond the graves of the distant past. He presumed they were family and it made him curious and a bit jealous. She had a history here—family—people who loved her. Aside from his mother, all he had was hate and fear and bad memories. He could never feel at home in this place.

She sniffled.

"Don't get all sad on me," he said gruffly. "You know I can't stay here."

"And why is that?" she said, her voice breaking.

"Well hell, for starters, I'm a murderer."

"Oh that…. Everyone knows Chester was a hothead. Even his wife said it was in self-defense."

"It was, but I could've maybe hit him softer you know."

She snuggled up against him and held his strong body tighter, speaking quietly in his ear.

"You were just a teenager, Jeremy, attacked by a grown man; you had to do what you did. There's no shame in surviving. Nobody holds it against you."

"And my stepdad. I hate that creep with all my guts. If I stick around here I just know that I'll end up like him, a small time pimp and pusher."

"You don't have to, you know."

"What?"

"Be like him. You can fight it. Make something positive out of your life."

"You almost make me think I could."

"Sure you could… I could help you."

"You don't know me. It's the darkness. It's in my nature."

Katy rolled onto her back and stared at the ceiling.

"It's like the Indians say," she said quietly. "You just have to feed the good wolf inside you, Jeremy and let the bad one starve."

"That ain't so easy," he snarled. "No, I think it's best I move on. Maybe go south."

Katy rolled over, and lay facing away from him in silence.

"You aren't mad at me are you?" he asked finally.

"No," she said softly and wiped away her tears.

CHAPTER TWENTY-THREE

"The boy is going with me, tonight and I'll have no argument from you."

Roy Sr. loomed menacingly over his tiny wife in the living room of their ranch home.

"But you know tonight's his dance class," she sputtered. "He's all excited. They are working on their Arabesques. You know he told me the other day he wants to be a *Danseur noble*."

"A what? I don't give a rat's ass what he's learning. It's bad enough you got him doing that girly dance crap. I am the laughingstock of the county thanks to that kid."

"Oh that isn't true, Roy, and he enjoys it—"

"Fuck that shit, prancing around like a sissy."

"—and it has improved his coordination so much... For sports, I mean."

"Well, that much is true I'll admit," the Sheriff grumbled, "and that is the only reason I even allow this nonsense to continue. But he can miss it this week. I want to spend some time with my son. Teach him the manly art of ice fishing at night."

"You aren't going to give him any beer, are you Roy? You know he has a delicate stomach."

"I don't know how something that big could be delicate. Don't know where he got that from. Neither one of us is fat."

"My sister had a glandular issue, maybe he's got it too. He's not fat you know, just a little chubby. He could grow out of it," she said nervously—trying not to remember another night shortly before the one when she first slept with Roy, Sr., and then told him she was pregnant. And the face and curly hair of another boy who was heavy-set and gentle and kind, but who left town the next day for college and never returned.

"He just needs more exercise," Roy Sr. lectured.

"Like dancing? He's already in football, baseball, hockey and basketball…what more can the poor boy do to satisfy you?"

"Ice fishing for starters. Junior!" he yelled. "Get your ass out here!"

Young Junior ran down the stairs and leaped into the room wearing tights. "Is it time to go? I can't wait to—"

"What in God's name!" Roy, Sr. sputtered. "Get those things off and change into your long johns—oh hell leave 'em on, but put some pants on over them. They'll work the same. Just don't let anybody see them. I'm taking you ice fishing tonight."

"But I have dance class, Dad. The teacher promised that we would be working on our Arabesques."

"You can work on whatever you are talking about next week. Just hurry up and get dressed and get your boots on, the guys are waiting."

"Well, Ok. Do I really get to go with you and the guys?"

"Yeah, it'll be real fun. More fun than a wimpy dance class, I promise. And if you're real good and behave yourself, I got a surprise for you later."

"Oh you boys," Junior's Mom tittered. "Well, enjoy yourselves and stay out of trouble."

As the truck drove down the icy road, Junior fidgeted in the passenger seat and amused himself by breathing on the window and drawing shapes in the moisture.

"Where are we going, Dad?" he asked.

"You'll see. We got a special place up here on Bone Lake," Roy Sr. replied gruffly. "It's more than just fishing son, It's a meeting and a bit of a party. You have to treat your people right. Make them want to work hard. Make them respect you."

The sheriff turned the truck down a side road that led down to the water's edge where a bonfire was burning on the shore under light flurries of sparkling snowflakes descending from a sky dotted with stars. Several ice fishing huts were erected on the surface of the lake and 15 to 20 men of all ages stood around the huts and the fire laughing and drinking.

As Roy Sr. pulled the truck into place, the men congregated around the fire and gave him their rapt attention as he and Junior climbed out and stomped through the drifts down to the fire.

"Hey Boss!" The men called out in greeting as the duo came closer.

"Hey boys, how're they biting?" he asked with a friendly wave.

"Not bad, Chief." Junior recognized his father's friend Big Sid's voice from one of the parka-clad men in the circle. "But the whiskey is better." Everyone laughed.

Roy Sr. grabbed the bottle offered and took a big swig.

"Yes! Now that's the good stuff. Say fellas, you all know my kid, Roy Jr. Why don't you take him out and show him the ropes— teach him what this ice fishing business is all about."

"Sure Boss, we'll take good care of him!"

A younger guy by the name of Lewis and a couple others dressed in heavy coats, mittens and wool caps grabbed Junior and pulled him along out onto the lake. Lew showed him how to use an auger to drill a hole in the ice, and a skimmer to clear the slush out of the hole. Then he showed him how to set up a tip-up, and bait the hook with a minnow and drop the line down the hole he had just drilled.

"So how long do we wait?" Junior asked excitedly.

"Oh we don't wait out here," Lew said with a grin. "Come on into the hut and we'll warm up a bit. We can fish some in there where there's heater and then come back and see if you caught anything out here."

"Sounds good," said Junior, who was feeling a bit chilled.

Once inside the hut, Lew, Junior and the other men sat down in the warm, womblike chamber and placed a couple lines down the hole in the ice inside. Sitting back to relax, Lew smiled and pulled a bottle of schnapps out and took a swig.

"Mmmm hmmm, try some Junior," the man offered the bottle to the boy. "It'll help warm you up."

"Oh no, I don't drink."

"Aw c'mon."

"I got a bad stomach—and I promised my mom."

Everyone laughed.

"He promised his mommy," one of the men chortled and slapped his knee.

"Shut up, dummy—this is the boss' son and we promised him we'd teach him what ice fishing is all about. Now come on Junior, this stuff will do you good, and it tastes sweet like candy."

Junior took the bottle and warily took a small sip. It had a kick, but he had to admit it did taste vaguely like candy. The first swallow went down hard, but the syrupy aftertaste lingered on his tongue and lips and the warmth filled his belly and he decided he wanted to taste it again. When he took the next sip and then a full swallow, the men in the hut cheered and slapped him on the back.

An hour later, after Lew had showed Junior how to jig the line and they had pulled a couple small crappies and a nice perch out of the chilly water, with another bottle emptied, they left the shanty to return to the hole where Lew showed Junior the lifted tip-up flag meant there is a fish on the line. They pulled out a couple of bluegills and another crappie to take back and show the old man.

The boy staggered back eagerly across the ice to the shore with the men to show his father his catch, but Roy Sr. shushed him. Sid gathered the men around the fire, telling them the boss was going to make an announcement. The sheriff cleared his throat and raised a glass of whiskey to the stars before speaking in a strong clear voice.

"Here's to the important things in life —family, friends and ice fishing," he said and took a drink, and everyone followed suit. "You are all an important part of my business—my family, and I am sure that none of us will ever forget this night. First off, I think we need to drink a toast to my son—Junior, take a bow. I hope someday he will grow up to be one of us and take his rightful place with us in our work."

The men cheered and slapped Junior's back and drank up again before Roy Sr. cleared his voice and continued.

"I think it is important to remember on this glorious occasion how we all have to work together in our efforts because as you know, neither God nor the government is ever gonna give you anything."

"You got that right!" shouted Sid, and everyone in the crowd laughed.

"No, you gotta take what you want in this sorry world. But how do you do it if you're all alone? Well, you can't, can you? That's why we all need to work together, because together we are strong and might makes right. We'd all be collecting welfare or working our asses off at some gas station or hardware store or, God forbid, in the mines, working for someone else, working for peanuts. No, with our work together we are important, we have goals, we have power. We have a great business that you are all an important part of, so be glad you are on the right side and fuck everyone else. This is our county!"

More drinking and vigorous cheers greeted this pronouncement. The Sheriff held up his hand for calm.

"But that is not the only reason we have to celebrate here tonight. You all remember when our friend Teddy, the little rat, stole the money he owed me from that business deal with Johnny Montaigne and then skipped town? Wasn't hard for us to figure out, his girlfriend admitted he bought a bus ticket to Seattle with it when we asked her nicely," he said with a grim chuckle.

"Wasn't a terrible amount of dough, but it kind of left a bit of a bad taste in my mouth and forced me to liquidate some inventory early just to meet the agreed-upon schedule. Hurt my pride a bit too, and that's just about the worst thing to do to a man is to cheat and rob and betray him when he trusts you, because a man's pride is just about the most important thing a man can have."

The large man paused. All eyes were on him as he spoke—the shadows on his face grew deeper in the flickering fire below.

"I have to admit that I am a proud man. I know it's a sin, but there you have it. Teddy boy hurt my pride and he caused me a little bit of inconvenience with his inconsiderate action. Don't know why he wanted to go there anyway, I could never stand a place where it rains all the time. Too damp—bad for your health. Well, me and Sid here, we have a few friends of our own out in the beautiful Pacific Northwest, so we made a call or two and, well let's just say it turned out the climate didn't agree with Teddy and they helped him find his way back home to us."

"Where is the creep, he owes me 20 bucks?" a shivering man called from the edge of the crowd.

"Yeah, he owes me too," another man agreed.

"Well sure, I'll let you boys have a chat with him if you'd like", Roy Sr. said, his eyes brightening. "Right now as a matter of fact. Hell, I'll even let my son here, do the honors. Junior, take a hold of that chain there and pull."

He pointed at a chain on the ice. Shakily, Junior bent over and picked it up.

"That's it—pull on it."

Junior felt sick—his stomach wasn't feeling so good after his numerous slugs of schnapps chased by beer, but all eyes were on him and he wanted to make his father proud, so he pulled the chain.

"That's it, pull harder, Roy. That's the way."

Junior pulled as hard as he could. The heavy chain led to a hole drilled in the ice and felt as though attached to a dead weight. He pulled with all his strength until something bumped up beneath the ice below. Everyone gathered around. Sid used his boot to sweep away the light dusting of snow on the ice surface as Lew moved his lantern nearer. Its light shone down brightly, revealing a man's body with weights attached to it floating in the water below and Teddy's battered and swollen face pressed up against the ice.

"I told you he wouldn't like the damp," the sheriff said coldly.

CHAPTER TWENTY-FOUR

"Sheriff."

Junior looked up from his cluttered desk in exasperation.

"What do you want, Deputy?'

"Looks like we got another one."

"What? Who, where?" Junior leapt to his feet scattering papers with his sudden motion.

"Old man Jorgenson," the deputy said breathlessly. "You know, out there down off of Power Plant Road a ways. You know. Just got a call, the meter reader says she saw him lying on the floor through the window."

"Christ! He's dead?"

"Says he ain't movin' any."

"Tell him to rap on the window."

"SHE says she's been rappin' but he just lies there all bug-eyed."

Junior pondered the new information for a few seconds.

"The meter guy, he see anybody else in the house?"

"SHE didn't say she did. She's still on the line. Wanted to know if SHE could leave—SHE still has quite a few houses to visit."

"Tell her yeah, ok, but be ready to come in and make a statement later this afternoon."

Junior stood up and put his gun belt on.

"C'mon Bobby, let's get ourselves out there quick before that damn kid gets out of the area."

The two men moved quickly out the door and climbed into the cruiser parked in the lot. The deputy steered the car out of the parking lot, down the road past the dam and headed out of town.

"Hell, now that we got lady meter readers peekin' through windows and all, boss, I guess I shouldn't watch the game in my underwear anymore, huh?"

"You do that?"

"Sometimes, well yeah. when I get hot."

"Thanks for sharing that with me, Deputy. I'm gonna have a hard time getting that picture out of my head."

They slowed down and pulled off the road into the driveway of a small cottage and parked the car. The deputy pulled out his gun and approached cautiously. He knocked on the door and called out, "Iron County Sheriff Department, open up." The deputy motioned that he was going to kick the door in, but .Junior stopped him and with a sneer on his face, simply turned the doorknob and opened the door.

The deputy advanced with gun drawn and began an exaggerated search of all the rooms as the Sheriff bent over the body on the floor.

"He's dead alright."

"All clear," the deputy shouted from the bedroom.

"You check the shower?"

"Humph, of course."

"What about that closet," the chief motioned.

"Huh? Oh dammit."

The deputy approached the hall closet and opened it. Something leaped out and the deputy fired his pistol into the interior."

Junior stood up and patted the deputy on the back as he stared into the dark interior.

"Congratulations Bobby, you nearly wounded that dangerous broom."

"Sorry Sheriff, think I oughta' patch that hole up or something?"

"Forget about it. Just hang a coat over it and no one will notice."

With a sigh, Junior knelt back down and checked the dead man for wounds.

"Hmmm"

"What's up, Sheriff?"

"No blood."

"You don't say? That's strange."

"Yup. Mighty peculiar. I don't see any bullet holes or stab wounds either."

"Hmmmm, ya don't suppose…"

"What?"

"Poison."

Junior looked up at the deputy, "You know Bobby, I sometimes find myself speechless when you display the depths of your mighty intellect."

"Thanks Boss," the deputy beamed.

"But, no. I'd say we just got ourselves a little false alarm here. Yeah, I'd say a heart attack's probably what got him."

"Christ, well at least it ain't that crazy kid anyhow."

"You ain't whistlin' Dixie."

Junior stood up, looked around the room and pointed.

"Lookie there, a bunch of crumbs on a plate on the couch."

"And an empty jar of pickles and mayonnaise spilled on the floor and counter," the deputy chimed in.

"Yup, the way I see it, the ol' man got up for a midnight snack and just…" Junior stuck his tongue out and mimed falling over.

"His wife's dead ain't she?" he asked as he straightened up.

"Oh for sure, Sheriff, she's been gone awhile now."

"Hmmmm."

"Yeah, hmmm."

Junior glanced around the room.

"Used to have a dog didn't he?"

The deputy's face brightened. "Yeah, I believe so."

"What kind of dog was that he had, a bassett—no a beagle?"

"Yeah, I think you're right, Boss."

"Yeah"

"Uh huh."

The men stood quietly for a moment before Junior broke the silence.

"Heck of a nice dog."

"They usually are."

"Uh huh."

"Yup."

The men continued looking around the room.

"Not so good around kids though."

"So I hear."

"His dog's dead I suppose?"

"Haven't seen it around for a while."

"Too bad."

"Yeah, it was a cute little thing."

"Yeah."

"Too bad."

"A shame."

Junior looked down at the dead man's contorted face. *Man, he looked scared to death.* he thought.*What did those eyes see as the reaper approached? Did his life flash past in ultra fast forward? Was it scary fun like a roller coaster into a void, or was it like falling off a haywagon onto a pitchfork out in a hayfield in the middle of nowhere and just kind of dangling there in the breeze with the life draining out of ya' kind of thing?* Junior shivered.

"Kind of yappy though… beagles are," the Sheriff said.

"So I hear."

"Well, I got'ta get back to the office. You stick around for the coroner, Bobby and catch a ride back with him. And… at least close his damn eyes, will ya'."

CHAPTER TWENTY-FIVE

"Do you ever think about what happened?"

The woman in the chair across from Jeremy shifted in her seat and looked up from her note pad.

"What do you think?" he said and his lips curled into a sneer.

"We're not here to discuss what I think, Jeremy."

"So why talk, we got a nice couch over there? Has anyone ever told you that you have pretty eyes?"

"I've actually been told my ass is my best feature. So you are a sweet talker, does that line ever actually work for you?"

"All the time."

"Really?" She raised an eyebrow.

"You don't believe me?"

"At the risk of offending, you I would guess you've maybe been to 2nd base... once. Am I right?" Jeremy sat silent.

"The day the incident occurred, you and your friends were buying beer illegally. What else did you plan to do?"

"You know, get wasted, hang out in the woods, maybe go swimming... the usual."

She scribbled some notes before continuing.

"So, you were leaving with the beer to go have a party and the bar owner showed up. What happened after that?"

"Jesus, haven't I already told this story a thousand fucking times already?"

"Last time, I promise."

"Oh right, I'm sure I'll be telling this story the rest of my life. Pretty sure about that."

"So the man approached. Was he angry?"

"You could say that."

"Can YOU say that?"

"Yes."

"He was mad about the beer?"

"Well he was mad. Yeah, he was all pissed and yelling. He hit one of the guys, Kyle I think. Some of the others ran off, the cowards."

"You don't like cowards do you?"

"Not really."

"So you had to stand up to... Mr. Jensen was it? To show the others?"

"I guess."

"Are you the leader, then?"

"What do you mean?"

"Do you make the decisions and the other boys follow you?"

"Yeah, I suppose they do."

"Do you enjoy that... being the leader?"

"Someone has to be I guess—either that we all just get old and die. Or you could end up sitting on your pretty ass in a chair asking a bunch of bullshit questions. I tell you what, lady—I got a question for you. Do they pay you anything worthwhile for this shit gig, or you just do it to pay for cat food for your cats?"

"You think I have cats?" She raised an eyebrow.

"I got you figured out. No ring on your finger. No family photos. You're one of those lonely broads who eat ice cream and read romance novels and work stupid jobs 'helping people.'"

"Wrong on most counts. I'm married, happily—don't wear the ring at work, it catches on things. I have two small kids, a boy and a girl. Don't have photos on my desk for space reasons, and I like to keep my personal life separate from my job. And I own a border collie. I'm a dog person."

108

"Fuck."

"Your hostility is exceeded only by the level of your misapprehensions. Can we try to limit the sarcasm and foul language and try to maintain a degree of respect during these sessions?"

Jeremy sat silently glaring.

"Well, I think we are done for today, but please think about what I said. You may have been wrong with most of your assumptions, but you were right about one thing—I am here to help you."

"You want to help me?"

"Yes, I truly do."

"Then show me your ass."

CHAPTER TWENTY-SIX

I awake to darkness and silence, hunger and pain.

I am still trapped and can't move my arms. My head is bruised and blood is matted in my hair.

I try to move and my ribs explode and I scream in my mind.

Help! I cry, but my lips are parched and no sound escapes them.

And no one answers.

CHAPTER TWENTY-SEVEN

"Of course you can use my office, "the Sheriff said sweetly before bellowing, "June, Mr. Taylor would like to talk to you," as he exited the room and went for a cup of coffee.

A chill went up Junior's back. He fumbled to put away some paperwork and had to remind himself to breathe as he glided into the Sheriff's office. Once inside, he faced the intense presence of Lance Taylor sitting in the chair behind the desk, backed by his black bodyguard who stood with folded arms to the side of the billionaire like a harem eunuch. Taylor looked up and smiled.

"Roy Pultz, Jr.? So, you're Junior? Think I remember meeting your old man... He was an asshole."

Junior tried not to smile. He kind of liked the rich bastard at the moment. At least he spoke his mind. And obviously a good judge of character. Of course, his money and power allowed him to say what he wanted without repercussions; Junior didn't have that status and might going for him; not yet anyway.

"Your boss tells me you were on duty the day the boys came through town. I know he's already asked you about this, but I like to look a man in the eyes when I ask him a question. And while I would usually just leave the matter to my friend here, I think Mr. Wheeler, despite his large and rather fearsome appearance, might be too nice a guy for this type of interview. I'm sure you realize, Pultz, that I'm not a nice guy. You don't get to where I am in life by pussyfooting around. So I am going to have you sit down right here and I'll look you in your face when I ask my questions. You don't mind, do you?"

"Not a bit, but keep it quick, I've got a ton of paperwork to finish up." Junior felt the heat rise to his cheeks.

"Paperwork huh? Ain't that a bitch? That's the trouble with this world these days, too many regulations, too much paper and not enough blood, sweat and tears. In fact, I'd venture to say those boys would probably be found and home safe in bed already if you all weren't sitting on your asses 'typing' like stenographers instead of out slogging through the woods with the dogs searching for those boys like real professionals would."

"I'm sure the Sheriff has filled you in on all the steps our department and the Crystal Falls police have taken," Junior replied, trying to stay calm in the face of the slew of insults being directed towards him, which he knew were designed to get under his skin. "We've done extensive reconnaissance of the town and the surrounding area—with a K-9 team I might add, and searched the campsites and forests and caves, and in the end have unfortunately concluded those boys are obviously nowhere in the county."

"Yes, I've talked to your boss and… frankly I have come away less than impressed with the man's… 'acuity.' I am not sure exactly what the crime statistics are around here in Mayberry, but I suspect your Sheriff has more than enough trouble just remembering if the mustard goes on the inside or the outside of the bread when he makes a sandwich, if you get my drift, Deputy Pultz."

"Uh." Junior started and then bit his lips.

"You know there have always been some rumors about this place," Taylor went on, "Iron County in general. They used to say people—quite often vagrants and those petty criminals operating on the wrong side of the law, had a tendency to… disappear around here. Lots of strange and mysterious vanishings reported when your father was around—all unsolved of course. And of course, there were those Hawkins brothers and the Peterson kid gone a few years ago without a trace. Makes one wonder —what do YOU think is going on, Deputy Pultz?"

Junior breathed deeply and spoke in measured tones, "Actually, the younger Peterson kid was determined to have committed suicide, and it was pretty clear the Hawkins clan and the Petersons were involved in some type of rivalry—"

"Over drugs, yes, yes." Taylor waved his hand dismissively. "And a questionable suicide. That's what they said I know, but my questions IS… if they killed each other off, which seems an unlikely and rather convenient scenario in my opinion—who was it exactly that was left standing? You see I'm a businessman,

'Junior,' and I know for a fact that nothing in life happens without winners and losers, and the winners always take the money and power from the losers. So, I ask you, if both of those two families lost… who took the money and filled the power vacuum when the Hawkins and Peterson gangs simply vanished into thin air? Somebody has to know where the bodies are buried, don't you agree?"

"Well, I admit that we do unfortunately have some issues with drugs around here," Junior answered dully, "but with so many people out of work, they have to find alternative ways to make money and spend their free time. The Iron County Sheriff's Department is working hard to clean up—"

"Cut the crap Pultz, I did a little research on your boss out there and it seems he's doing pretty well for himself in these hard times. That new Escalade he's driving, the cabin on the lake, the boats and snowmobiles and all that jewelry he's been giving his wife seem to add up to more than his official salary—quite a bit more I'd say. Now, I don't begrudge a man making his living—honest or not, and if he's able to keep our commie government's greedy hands out of it, well more power to him. But you should know that I have friends. And you and your boss probably wouldn't want to meet my friends because they're the kind of guys who thought it was fun to napalm villages of women and children in Vietnam and I'm sure they'd love nothing more than to turn this little hamlet into a burning graveyard."

"If I had seen the boys I'm sure I would remember them, but I didn't see them like I told you before."

"No, you were probably busy eating doughnuts, ogling porn or taking a dump or whatever you do when you aren't doing any real police work." Taylor's eyes burned with hatred as he grew increasingly angry and he stared into Junior's eyes as he spat out his venom.

"You know you don't look much like your dad. No… no, he was a tough guy, a real hard ass; he'd look you in the eyes without blinking and dare you to say something. You must take after your Mom, right—soft and doughy. She must be a real prize—"

Junior leapt to his feet and drew back his fist.

"Shut the fuck up or I'll—"

Wheeler stepped forward, but Taylor gestured for him to stop.

"No, Mr. Wheeler, don't interfere. Deputy Pultz should know how much I love suing people and ruining their lives, and I might add that of course I never lose. But I am impressed Pultz. Was that an unexpected show of... spunk? Perhaps you do have some of your father in you after all... his temper, perhaps? So now the question comes to mind that if you were willing to hit a distraught and defenseless old man for merely asking questions about a lost child, what would you have possibly done with a smart mouth teen age, drag-racing, thief or two? Yes, I know my son has quite the mouth on him—he takes after me I'm afraid, and after all, he and his friend had crossed the line of civil behavior with their unfortunate prank at the gas station. Maybe, in an overzealous attempt at upholding the law—in teaching them a... lesson, things went too far...?"

"Taylor, first things first. Leave my mom out of any of this. You don't know her." Junior's face was crimson and he could barely suppress a sob from emerging from his chest as he spoke. "My mother is an angel and you don't deserve to even speak of her with that sewer hole of a mouth of yours. As for your punk son, quite honestly I couldn't care less if he's ever found. It's my job and I do it to my best abilities, but it is obvious to me that he was more than likely just a spoiled, selfish waste of breath with no sense of decency—just like his father. He and his pal probably stole the beer and headed over to the Res to see if they could find a squaw to have a little fun with and ended up getting caught by her brothers. Yes, he's a missing person and I'll keep looking for him like I am supposed to, but I have plenty of other responsibilities keeping me busy doing my job protecting the citizens of this county. I will not let some rich asshole bully me into spending all of my time finding his lost drugged-out loser of a son."

"Well now, that's interesting," the rich man hissed, while learning forward and folding his well-manicured fingers together. "Were the boys on drugs when you saw them last?"

"They're all on drugs these days, you stupid shit. Now why don't you and your goon fuck off!"

"I like your spirit, Deputy." Taylor leaned back. "Underneath your harmless looking exterior burns the rage of a lion. Well, we are, as you helpfully suggested, making a short visit to the reservation tomorrow. A large contribution to the tribe's casino expansion has opened their eyes to working with us in determining whether the boys were foolish enough to stray somewhere where they were not wanted. But be assured, 'Junior,' that we will be back soon. Very soon. You clowns may not agree, but time is of the essence. And when I return, I would be most interested in spending some more time with you and maybe we will find the opportunity to go over, step by step, just exactly what you did on that day when the boys first crossed in to Iron County and arrived in the godforsaken town of Crystal Falls."

CHAPTER TWENTY-EIGHT

The months dragged on for what seemed like an eternity, but for Adele, the wait was worth it as the winter dance was the event of the year. In fact, the party, in the newly built addition to the Methodist Church, was considered to be the most exciting and joyous occasion to have taken place in the brief history of Mansfield.

The church usually frowned on such frivolous celebration, but the preacher was persuaded by the heartfelt entreaties of the townsfolk and ultimately relented in exchange for a promise of a full house for his Christmas sermon, and the evening was a true success, brimming with communal spirit and good cheer. There was dancing and music along with food and punch—which some of the men managed to spike, causing howls of derision and condemnation from the Preacher's wife. But even her complaints were drowned out by the vivacity of the revelers and the good will expressed by the Finns, Italians, Swedes and Cornish families as they forgot about their hardships and the howling storm outside long enough to make merry.

Adele's father was the star of the evening, as he and the other Cornish musicians played and sang sad songs about missing their homeland. Adele had never been prouder of her papa, who looked so handsome in his soft red curls and beard as he showed his dexterity on the fiddle until early in the morning.

Her little sisters and brothers were jealous that she got to attend. She danced with her friends and her older brother and, yes, with the handsome Finnish boy who fulfilled his promise and arrived with the gift of a rose that he had hand carved. And yes, he held her in his arms that night, and softly professed his love for her, if you really must know.

The rest of the winter and early spring were long, dark and arduous and Adele thought her heart would break during the long days when she did not see the boy that by now everyone in town was calling her sweetheart. He worked long hours in the mines and was often too tired during the day to go for a walk with her or visit the family. He would make a point of going to church Sunday mornings with her, although his family were Lutherans, but he would often fall asleep during the service, so they decided it was better to just invite him over for Sunday dinner.

Adele's mother and the younger children adored Johnny, and he had always been friends with her older brother Ken—only her father remained wary of the young man, who tried his best to impress Adele's father by working hard at the mine and keeping an eye out for Ken. By the time summer was encroaching, Johnny felt he had softened the man's heart enough to humbly ask her father for her hand. The man's heart was saddened as he sucked on his pipe and thought hard with tears in his eyes about the girl who had played on the deck of a ship crossing the Atlantic and who had seemingly grown up into a woman when he blinked his eyes. She was always his favorite to hold and cuddle on his knee and now she would sit on another man's knee and he would hold her in his arms no more. But he knew that Johnny, despite being a Finn, was a hard worker who obviously loved his daughter as much as she loved him, so with voice cracking, he gave them his benediction. The date was set for June and Adele now lay in her bed at night dreaming of her new life as a wife.

Her dreams were interrupted one night in May when alarm went off at the mine, and her fears were realized. She and her mother and the other wives and mothers ran to the edge of the mine area, but were stopped by the guard.

"No women!" he shouted sternly. "Keep back!"

"What happened?" They asked. "Please tell us."

The guard softened. "There was an explosion and someone was hurt," he replied.

"Who was it? Was he hurt bad?" they pleaded with the guard for any additional information, but he said he none to give and they would just have to wait to see.

The women worriedly stood their ground, weeping and waiting for the news of whose son, husband, father or uncle had been taken this time, while trying to comfort and console each other.

Panicked, Adele ran back home and hurriedly put on a pair of her brother's pants and coat and tucked her hair under a cap before turning and racing back to the mine.

The guard waved the 'young man' who was coming to help the rescue through, and Adele approached the entrance in time to see the skip emerge from the depths carrying several grimy and bloodied men. Her eyes darted across the faces, but she did not see her father, her brother or Johnny.

The men clambered out of the bucket and another group rushed in. Without a second thought, Adele climbed in as well. The bell rang and with a lurch the skip lowered into the dark recesses below.

Adele held her breath as the skip descended down the shaft past several levels. The men in packed the skip around her, wondered out loud what had befallen and expressed concern for which of their coworkers may have been involved. Moving deeper into the earth, the air grew cold and damp and filled with dust and strange fumes. The darkness was lit only by candle light and men's shouts, furious clanging and distant water dripping could be heard in the depths of the darkness. She had never been down below before and could only imagine what it must be like to spend half your life working underground: it was like working in hell.

The bucket stopped abruptly and swayed as the men quickly climbed out and ran into the drift. Adele closed her eyes as she jumped out, knowing that if she fell it could be hundreds of feet down into the blackness.

Adele's heart beat louder and faster and her mind raced as she rushed with the men down the tracks—ducking under overhanging planks, swerving around rubble and ore cars that nearly blocked the path that led down the cavern tunnel to where the shouts were loudest. Reaching a spot where another smaller supply shaft came down to the drifts from the surface they saw a group of miners kneeling around a prone body. Adele worriedly scanned the men and saw her father and Johnny, and then suddenly realized that the body on the ground had to be her brother. She cried out in anguish, "Ken!"

"Adele?" her father mumbled as he looked up, startled to see her. She turned to Johnny who knelt beside him.

"I'm sorry Adele," the boy said quietly.

Her father sadly explained what had happened. "There was an explosion that shook the ground. Ken was high on that ladder getting us some lumber and when the ground shook, the rung came loose and…"

Adele stared at her brother's crumpled body and wailed—her piercing cry reverberating through the shaft and tunnels.

Men came running. One tore the cap off of Adele's head. There was a gasp from several in the gathering as her long red hair fell out.

"A woman!"

"And red hair to boot!"

"It's bad luck," one hissed and the men stepped back as though the girl was a hot iron. Johnny leapt to his feet.

"I'll take her home," he said and ushered the crying girl quickly down the passageway and back to the lift bucket.

Adele's eyes were downcast and she seemed to be in a daze as her fiancé lifted her gently and carried her into the lift. As he did, she mouthed the words over and over: "You promised."

CHAPTER TWENTY-NINE

They walked leisurely along the paved path, Jeremy pushing the wheelchair and Katy walking alongside as Preacher, the man from Room 207, gazed in wonderment at his surroundings and a smile that never seemed to end broke out across his face.

Truly the light is sweet, and a pleasant thing it is for the eyes to behold the sun

"Trees, sunlight, the wind blowing off the river… I never thought I would see it again. I almost feel alive again."

"How long has it been?" Katy asked.

"Well, let's see… it's been forever."

"So you knew my Mom, right Mr. LaPointe?"

"Oh Jeremy, let him enjoy his day out."

"No it's okay. And you can call me Nate… or Preacher. I did know your mom—she was one of my best friends when we were growing up. We used to hang out under the bridge right over there."

"You mean, over there?" Katy raised her arm and pointed and laughed. "That was one of my hangouts growing up too, although it was more a place for the "burnouts?""

"The druggies?" Jeremy turned red. "I practically lived under there. Is it still the same, I wonder?"

"Don't think it ever changes," Katy said smiling, "But, we'd have to push Mr. LaPointe through the grass to get there, and…" she squinted at the shadows where she thought she saw movement," I think someone might be under there already."

"Yeah, better skip it," Jeremy replied. "Probably bring back bad memories anyway."

But if a man live many years, and rejoice in them all; yet let him remember the days of darkness; for they shall be many. All that cometh is vanity.

"Your mother... Preacher began, "I don't know if you know it, but she had a... rough life."

"She's never really said anything about it. What do you mean? Because of my dad, or what? I know her mother was a crazy Bible-thumper, but—"

"We were together one night under that bridge, when she first told me... just how bad it was."

"She had it tough, huh?"

Preacher watched the river for a moment before going on.

"Her stepfather, Red, was one of the worst people I ever saw. Don't know exactly what he did to her, but it can't have been good. He was pretty infamous for poisoning dogs as a hobby. And, her mother, well... Jenny showed me the welts on her back."

"Her own mother beat her?" Katy gasped.

Preacher nodded

"No wonder she wouldn't let Junior lay a hand on me," Jeremy said thoughtfully.

"And then of course, Jesse—your dad, disappearing...

Preacher watched as a small blue butterfly flitted around his head before landing on his arm and he almost smiled. But then, as if in pain, he closed his eyes. and when he spoke again, his voice was soft and choked with emotion.

"You know that she was riding with me the night this happened to me."

"Shit, I had no idea. That is terrible. Does she ever visit you?"

"No...well...just once. I don't think she could forgive me... for hurting us both so bad through my... actions."

"I'm so sorry, Mr. LaPointe," Katy said and wiped away a tear.

"Yeah, that's a real drag," Jeremy added.

"That's alright, I'm sure she had her hands full raising you."

"And you knew my dad too, didn't you?"

121

The smile faded. "Yes, I knew your dad too," he said softly as he remembered Jesse's face as he buried him on the lonely island in the middle of the Michigamme Reservoir. "He was my best friend."

"They said they never found out what happened to him. Heard he might've been caught by some bad guys down in Green Bay. That what you think?"

"Could be," Preacher said thoughtfully. "Yes, that's probably what happened."

"Well, I wanted to ask…You heard my mom's gone missing."

"No," Preacher was startled. "Jenny's gone? I didn't—what happened?"

"They think—" Katy started, but Jeremy interrupted impatiently.

"Junior says she's just hiding trying to make him look bad for the election, but I've got a bad feeling. Do you think the prick could've pulled some shit? With my mom, I mean."

Preacher's eyes widened and he spoke carefully. "You know as well as anyone what he's like. He's capable of anything."

In his mind, Preacher rose from his chair, pursued and vigorously strangled the fat Sheriff. In reality he could only imagine what it would be like to run, to move his arms again and to tighten his fingers around Junior's throat and squeeze.

"If he has hurt her…" he said finally, gasping emotionally as he spoke, and his broken body suddenly began convulsing violently, as he was lost to the hell of his eternal frustration.

CHAPTER THIRTY

"Larry, did the Finn pay you yet?" Junior said with a snort and looked up from the packages of drugs spread across the table in front of him.

"Yup. Every penny."

Larry stood in the corner of the cabin with a beer in his hand, his hard face expressionless. The other men in the room ranged in ages from their early twenties to their sixties. Having just finished unloading a shipment, they lounged around the room drinking and smoking.

"Good, good. Leave it in the box on your way out." Junior motioned to an open strong box on the table where bundles of bills were stacked within. Larry reached in his pocket and pulled out the money and placed it in the box. "So where'd he get the dough anyway?" Junior asked. "Thought he was pleading poverty."

"Somebody loaned him the money." Larry stated in a monotone voice. "Guess they're getting a nice rate on it too."

"Really, who was it?"

"Me."

The group of men laughed. Junior shook his head and smiled.

"Ha—smart guy. Hope he doesn't burn you."

"I know where he lives."

"Yeah I guess you do, since you're banging his wife."

Laughter again filled the room. Larry glared.

"He says he's going to sell his truck," Larry said flatly, with his eyes downcast.

"Ha, that'll be the day. He loves that thing more than he loves her," Junior chortled.

"If he doesn't pay me, I'll take the truck as trade."

"The wife too?"

"Why buy the cow?"

The men laughed in agreement.

"You got that right." Junior stopped testing the purity of the white powder on the table and looked up seriously," And speaking of which… Curly's been having a discipline problem with a couple of the girls at the ranch. You and John stop by and give him a hand, okay?"

"With pleasure, boss," skinny John said, leaping to his feet.

"Just, don't leave any marks—it's bad for business."

"Awww," John said and slumped back down in his chair.

"We got a shipment coming in from the Canadians Tuesday," Junior announced, "and a load of that good Mexican shit to be picked up next week down in Green Bay, so don't plan on any vacations. We'll need all hands on deck during our busy season.

"Damn I love Christmas, what with all the love and sharing and 'snow'." The Sheriff slapped a bag of cocaine on the table and everyone laughed again.

"Oh, oh… it's the law," sneered Larry as the door opened and a uniformed Deputy strode in.

"Chief…"

"What is it, Deputy?"

"Can we speak in private?"

"Sure, sure. You guys go do something useful for a change."

The men muttered and jostled each other as they broke the meeting up and dispersed into the night

"Spit it out, Bobby," Junior said, while locking the strongbox.

"It's your kid," the deputy said quietly.

"I don't have a kid," the Sheriff snapped.

"Your wife's kid, then."

"Jeremy, what about him?"

"Well, don't get mad, but… there was a party over in Iron River and a bunch of kids got busted. Jeremy was one of them. They didn't know who he was. Apparently he was carrying a knife and some reefer…"

"Christ."

"Police officer just gave me a call. They didn't book him yet and figured you could just go pick him up kind of under the radar."

"Shit, that kid never learns. I had to pull his ass out of trouble buying speed over on the Res two months ago."

"Maybe you're busy. I could get your wife—"

"No, don't say a word to Mrs. Pultz, Bobby. Keep this under your hat and I'll be sure you get a little extra in your Christmas bonus this year."

"Thanks sir. You want me to ride with you to go get him?"

"Thanks, no, you've done enough. This is my problem."

The Sheriff drove through the snow like a man possessed, windshield wipers busily pushing away the large flakes of snow that quickly accumulated, tires slipping on the icy corners. He was tempted to put on his flashing lights, but traffic on the highway was light, and he dreaded any attention that might bring another Jeremy 'incident to light,' so he simply plowed ahead, cursing all the while to himself.

Arriving at the police station in Iron Mountain in deep darkness, Junior entered and made the arrangements to free the wayward youth, who moped his way, still wearing handcuffs, into the car, where he was given the third degree from his stepfather.

"Alright you stupid punk, what the hell is wrong with you?"

"Fuck off," the boy muttered.

"I should have left you in jail. That's where you belong."

"Ha, Mom would get me out."

"You may have your mother fooled, but not me."

"Yeah, wait until she sees me come home in handcuffs. I'll have the last laugh then."

"You think this is a joke, creep?"

"As funny as your face when she finds out."

"Yeah funny. You're a real funny kid, you know that? You remind of somebody I used to know. He thought he was funny too. So funny that he went out for a drive one night and nobody ever saw him again. Because you know what? What is funny to you, is not so funny to other folks and some of them just might take offense one day to your particular brand of humor."

"You talking about my dad?"

"Smart kid. You know, you look just like him right now glaring at me like that. I know you want to kill me, but you don't have the balls. Are you really too stupid to realize this is my town, my county, and I run things around here, and I can't have my idiot stepson acting up and causing trouble. I can't have it. So..."

Junior turned off the highway and headed down a backroad.

"Where are you taking me? Aren't we going home?"

"We got a little stop to make."

Junior turned on the brights, but the snow was falling thickly now and simply reflected the glare, so he switched back. The road was not plowed, and his car nearly slid off the road as he spun his wheels along through the drifts piled high in wind-created crested waves across the pavement.

"Ow, watch you're driving, you're gonna kill us," the boy whined from the back after hitting his head against the window when the car slid hard with bump into and out of a ditch.

"I should be so lucky," Junior replied through gritted teeth.

At the end of a dead street, Junior parked and walked the kid roughly through the thick snow, pausing momentarily at the septic tank, covered by drifting snow, before entering the abandoned house through the back door.

"What the fuck are we doing here?" Jeremy complained.

"Shut up get down those stairs."

Down in the basement, Junior forced the boy into a chair and cuffed his wrists and ankles in place.

"I can't have you running around wild and can't afford to keep you in jail, although jail is certainly where a druggie loser like you belongs. I've run out of patience, so let's just lock you up here until you learn your lesson."

"Bullshit, you can't leave me here. Mom will kill you when she finds out."

"Oh you won't tell her, because I won't let you out if you do."

"Alright I won't tell her."

"No, sorry, but I don't believe you. I can hear the snotty sounds of sarcasm in your voice and I have experienced enough of your lies already in my life. You promised to stay out of trouble after I got you out of that trouble with the tribe, and just see how well that turned out. No, I think a few days by yourself, in solitary so to speak, to think about things, is just what you need."

"You can't leave me out here in the woods. It's fucking cold and the floor is wet. I'll get sick. I'll die of thirst or freeze to death."

"You're warming my heart with your sweet talk. Wouldn't that be just the best Christmas present ever? No. You'll be okay, kid, probably... I'll turn on that space heater before I go. Won't get real warm in here, but you won't freeze to death. Just sit tight and I'll be back after the new year. Have fun and enjoy Christmas, but hate to tell you, Santa ain't coming this year."

"You can't get away with this, you bastard."

"Such a foul mouth on you. Don't you know that that kind of talk gets you nowhere in life? And yes, I believe I can get away with this. Go ahead and scream. This is my house and my property. Nobody can hear you. Some of the other guys we've had out here have tried. Lord, they've tried real hard. Had to wear earplugs a few times it got so loud."

"Let me go. Let me go. My mother will find me—" Jeremy struggled at his bonds, as Junior made his way to the door.

"Naw, kids run away. All of the time. Some of them never come back either. She'll just think you decided to take off for a while, to cool off a bit. Besides, she doesn't even know about this place, so... see you in a few days... maybe. And let's work on that attitude a bit, OK champ?"

"Bastard! Bastard!"

"Sorry buddy, I have to turn off the lights now. We have to keep the power bills low now don't we?"

He started to reach for the light switch, but paused as he thought of something.

"Oh I just remembered, don't be afraid if you hear some little scratching sounds or feel a little nibbling. We've got a real rat problem in this place. Haven't had a chance to get an exterminator out here yet. Well, not for the rats anyway. But the little buggers breed like crazy and they'll eat just about anything, or so they tell me. But just... Oh you'll figure it out. Sleep tight, Jeremy."

Junior turned off the light and shut the door as Jeremy started to panic.

CHAPTER THIRTY-ONE

I called upon thy name, O Lord, out of the low dungeon.

When I say, My bed shall comfort me, my couch shall ease my complaint;

Then thou scarest me with dreams, and terrifiest me through visions:

So that my soul chooseth strangling, and death rather than my life.

I am afraid of all my sorrows, I know that thou wilt not hold me innocent.

I remember a time. There were the three of us: Jenny, with her golden hair blowing in the wind, Jesse with his face shining and… he had the biggest grin and me. What was it that particular day? Was it when we stole apples from the orchard and ate them until we puked. Or the time we gave Jesse's brother, Jake some money to buy us some schnapps? And we puked.

Jake, the same brother I had killed—well both brothers really—Jake in the ambush I set for him and Jared with the Spanish Pharaohs down in Green Bay—while the wretched beast Jared was killed by Junior out at Finn Town and fed to the wolves. Big Pete was killed that day at the ghost town too, and that is probably my fault as well, but that is all another story from another time.

And of course, I also nearly killed Jenny. Guess everyone who came near me met a sad fate in those days.

Behold, and see if there be any sorrow like unto my sorrow, which is done unto me, wherewith the Lord hath afflicted me in the day of his fierce anger.

From above hath he sent fire into my bones, and it prevaileth against them: he hath spread a net for my feet, he hath turned me back: he hath made me desolate and faint all the day.

So what was Jesse smiling for? He was always smiling, like a ray of sunlight on a stormy day—except for when his dad whupped him, or later when the drugs made him jealous and mean, but this time, his eyes were lit up like never before.

Wherefore is light given to him that is in misery, and life unto the bitter in soul;

Was it when I first told him about that buried treasure — that heap of gold bars from a train robbery I read about that, turned out to be a just a handful of rotting bills stashed under a rock? Or was it when he first kissed Jenny and she kissed him back—and I wanted to hide under a rock in jealousy? Or was it just before I smashed his face in with a rock…?

Which long for death, but it cometh not; and dig for it more than for hid treasures;

No, no, not that night. Never again that night…

Let me remember better times—those happier days when we roamed the woods and waters, the three of us floating along the current of the Paint River like white clouds drifting in a clear blue sky.

He turned to me with a smile so wide. What was he smiling for? Remember, Nate; remember, Preacher. Try….

Oh yes, it was that day.

Jesse's eyes danced and his face glowed in the moonlight, reflected off the ripples of the river as the three of us sat under the bridge and passed the joint between us. He hugged us both and kissed Jenny on the lips and nearly floated away into the starry sky in happiness, as he told us his secret.

They had come in the night, he said. He heard them breaking down the door and shouting. Federal agents.

Jude was passed out drunk, but when he came to, he fought them with all his might. It took four men to get the cuffs on and drag him out to the waiting car.

They found the guns and ammo. They found the heroin. They found the stash of money Jesse's father Jude had skimmed while working for Junior's dad. They found the hidden room behind the bookcase; they knew exactly where to look.

When they realized what was happening, Jesse's mother and brothers fought with the agents too, until an armed officer finally locked them in the basement, but Jesse avoided the fray and watched out the window as his father was beaten and carried away, shouting and screaming curses.

He would never forget. He explained how his father raised his bruised and angry face from within the back of the car and saw his son watching him. And he knew.

Jude would die the following year in prison in a prison fight that Junior's dad had arranged as a reward for his disloyalty. He would die fighting as the group of men surrounded him and stabbed him without mercy. He died as he lived, in violence, angry at the knowledge that his son had been the one to turn him in, but smiling and, in a way, proud of his son's action-as the life seeped away from him, his blood pooling around his body as he lay prone on the cold tile floor.

Sending his sadistic father to his death, Jesse tasted freedom. And Jesse tasted power. And our fates were sealed.

He never felt guilt, or if he did, he never mentioned it. His killer, however… is not granted such peace…

Let the day perish wherein I was born, and the night in which it was said, There is a man child conceived.

Let that day be darkness; let not God regard it from above, neither let the light shine upon it.

Let darkness and the shadow of death stain it; let a cloud dwell upon it; let the blackness of the day terrify it.

As for that night, let darkness seize upon it; let it not be joined unto the days of the year, let it not come into the number of the months. Lo, let that night be solitary, let no joyful voice come therein.

Let them curse it that curse the day, who are ready to raise up their mourning.

Let the stars of the twilight thereof be dark; let it look for light, but have none; neither let it see the dawning of the day:

I should have been as though I had not been; I should have been carried from the womb to the grave.

CHAPTER THIRTY-TWO

"Best Christmas ever…"

"Your mother?"

"She never came. I kept waiting for her. Hour after hour in the dark. I was cold and lonely and hungry and scared. I knew that if she ever needed me, I'd have come. But then I needed her and called her name over and over in my mind and… nothing. Why didn't she hear me? Why didn't she realize what happened and force the information out of her husband and come and find me?"

"When did he finally let you out?"

"A couple days later and I remember every second of it. I was terrified he would do it again, only the next time… He made me promise I wouldn't tell my Mom. I had to tell her I was staying at a friend's house and the phones weren't working in the storm."

"That's… horrible, Jeremy. Well, that explains some of your animosity toward your stepfather."

"You don't know the worst of it."

"Maybe another session. For now, when we met last, you were telling me about the day of the incident—"

"You mean when I killed that motherfucker? Thought you said I didn't have to talk about it anymore?"

"You didn't finish the story. You left off with Chester Jensen striking one of your friends?"

"Yeah, knocked Kyle on his ass."

"Then what?"

"I don't really remember?"

"Did Mr. Jensen try to take the beer?"

"Yeah, yeah he did. He took it in fact. He had a big fit that Betty sold it to us."

"Betty was his wife?"

"Yeah, they owned the bar."

"Why did she sell you the beer?"

"Ha, we lied and told her we were eighteen and had just joined the Army and were shipping out."

"That worked?"

"A couple times Then she found out. I think someone narc'd us out—maybe my asshole stepdad."

"Your stepdad the sheriff?"

"That's the one."

"So Mr. Jensen took the beer. How did that make you feel?"

"How do you think? We paid for it fair and square and he just smacked Kyle like that and took it. What a prick."

"So what happened then?"

"It's kind of hard to remember… I know he was yelling and threatening us and Betty. Then he threw the beer against the wall outside of the bar and smashed it all over. When he got really mad, the other guys took off."

"Sounds like a volatile situation. Mr. Jensen was from all accounts unstable and a rather large and violent man. Why didn't you run with the other boys?"

"He wouldn't give our money back."

"Was it a lot of money?"

"It was to us?"

"But was it worth risking an escalation of the situation over…" she checked her notes, "less than $20?"

Jeremy sat in silence.

"Then what happened? Did Mr. Jensen hit you?"

"More than that!"

"It says here he kicked you in the face and broke your nose?"

"The fucker sucker punched me. Had me looking the other way and then grabbed me by the fucking hair and... he used to be a kick boxer I hear. Not a very good one, but... good enough I guess."

"That had to hurt. I'm surprised it didn't knock you cold."

"It did. I was out for .... just a few seconds, I think. When I came too, I was bleeding all over and barely knew where the fuck I was."

"So you were disoriented?"

"Try taking a size 14 steel toed logging boot to your face and tell me how you'd feel."

"I believe you. So do you remember what happened next?"

"I'm sure it's all in your notes. He was standing over me and screaming and kicking me in the ribs."

"He broke three of your ribs, is that right?"

"Felt like more than that. More like a shotgun blast in my side."

"Go on."

"That's all there is."

"But..."

"I don't remember the rest."

"Jeremy, you have to trust me. These sessions are for your benefit and my reports will assist in confirming the decision to return you to society upon your 18th birthday. Unfortunately, your record is filled with 'incidents,' multiple reports of fights and other violent outbursts, petty theft, a stolen car situation, vandalism and many more issues. But clearly in this case you were threatened by a man who was much older and larger than you, and who had a long record of deploying violent tendencies. I believe you are basically a good kid who found himself in a bad situation. I don't believe you are a killer."

Jeremy looked up.

135

"That's where you are wrong, doc," he said softly while staring her in the eyes. "That's exactly what I am."

CHAPTER THIRTY-THREE

The kid watched the trio from his secluded spot under the bridge. The young blonde guy pushed the old cripple in the wheelchair along the path in the park toward the river, while the good looking, dark-haired girl walked along beside them—her hands moving busily as she spoke. The boy pressed himself deeper against the concrete wall and into the shadows as they advanced slowly toward him. He hoped they wouldn't see him, but if they did, he was ready. The guy pushing the chair looked pretty tough, but he didn't look as big when he viewed him through the scope of his rifle.

They didn't seem to see him, so he moved forward to watch them more closely and make his plans. He was going to have to leave soon anyway—maybe once it got dark—too many people knew about this place. He'd already had to take care of one problem that evening. If they came any closer, he'd be forced to make a decision.

Mentally, he went through the calculations: *shoot the man first; the woman would probably freeze and he could nail her with the next shot. The cripple would be easy pickings after that. Hell, maybe he'd let him be—he looked like he had enough problems as it is. No, better not leave any witnesses—might be better to put him out of his misery. He could take him with the first shot—the others might not notice right away, or think he's having a heart attack or something. Of course, the girl might scream, and that would be a drag, so maybe her first? The guy looked kind of wild and might*

137

come charging toward me and that would be an easy kill. There was so much to consider…

But he was bothered about the gunshots: the sound would give his location away and his being pretty much in the center of town, the cops would show up quickly and he might be dead before he could shoot them all and get the hell out. Damn, now he really wished he could have talked his mother into buying the silencer he really wanted for Christmas last year. He could have killed the whole town like he wanted to and no one would have even noticed.

The three turned toward the bridge and moved forward. The young woman suddenly raised her arm and pointed directly toward where the boy was standing. He fell back against the cold concrete wall, slid to a prone position on the ground and assumed a stable position and aimed, his body and mind tensed and in sharp focus on his prey.

The man in the wheelchair suddenly started choking and convulsing—eyes wide in terror. The woman knelt and attended to him and spoke some words rapidly to the young man, who turned the chair and hurriedly pushed it back toward the van.

The boy watched with empty eyes as they drove away and then returned to his spot sitting on a tattered sleeping bag next to the still warm body of a vagrant whose eyes were closed and throat was cut. Tim slipped quietly down the bank to the water's edge, dragging the man's lifeless body on top of the sleeping bag, which he set afloat downstream. He watched as it drifted away downstream in the current and then bent down to clean the blood from his hunting knife in the gloomy Paint River.

CHAPTER THIRTY-FOUR

Yeah, well I'm pretty shaken up about it myself. I'm just your average Joe—a typical guy from Indiana, a Hoosier through and through. I never thought I'd be one of those folks featured on one of those '*Unsolved Mystery*' type of things. But see, me and the wife were up here visiting relatives—her's ya' know. And I just don't really care much for her cousin Gus.

Oh, I shouldn't have said that, him being family and all, but you know he gives me the creeps with all his 'global warming is a plot to take away our guns' and borderline white supremacist stuff all the time, so I started thinking of ways to kind of get out and away from the family for a bit.

The house is just too darn tiny for all of us anyway, I get the claustrophobia big time, especially with Gus sermonizing and all that sauerkraut smell and all the dogs on the furniture and their awful cheap beer. I mean, I like beer myself, but that stuff tastes like cat pee, but then they get all weird if you bring your own, like you think you're too good for 'em, so I usually just suffer and eat too much sauerkraut and lutefisk and drink too much of that crap beer and then I feel sick to stomach for days.

Oh, where was I? Well, just around the time before we were going make the trip up here, I saw an advertisement in *Popular Mechanics* for one of those metal detector things, and I thought, hey, that might just be the ticket to get away from the wife's relatives for a bit.

Please don't tell her I said that, will ya? I'd always wanted one of those things when I was a kid. Wanted to go out West and find the Lost Dutchman Mine, but wouldn't you know it, I never even made it further than Kansas City and that was just a couple nights for a convention. The wife isn't much for traveling, she's more of a homebody and well, we got kind of stuck raising kids and never did get to see much of the world. Not that I have any regrets, especially seeing all that violence you see on TV, heck we got enough of it already right back home in Indiana, we don't need to go anywhere else to find any more.

But, as I was saying, I got the bug to do a bit of treasure hunting. I mean, the U.P.'s got a pretty wild history and there was mining there back in the day, I'm pretty sure. So I lied and told the family I was going fishing and naturally Gus wants to show me the best spots, but fortunately for me his gout's acting up so he can't go with me. Hallelujah! The younger cousins are all more into their video games then fishing. Gus insisted I use his canoe, so I got stuck with him dropping me off at the Michigamme Reservoir and I started paddling off like I know what I'm doing and he says he'll pick me up in six hours.

I'm not a novice at fishing, and I used to paddle a mean canoe back in my Scoutmaster days, but my main plan was just to head out and find a spot to start digging, but after a while, I kind of got into the whole lake-canoeing-under-the-sun thing again, and once I got my second wind, I felt like Hiawatha or something and ended up coming upon this island and thought, what the heck, maybe some pirates buried their treasure here. Not 'Yo Ho' pirates, but you know what I mean. As good a place as any to dig around a bit anyway.

I beached the boat and pulled out the metal detector and shovel—I had a heck of a time hiding those from that nosy Gus, but then he's half blind anyway, and I started scoping the island out. Had a bit of trouble getting the thing to work at first—new machine and all, but then I kind of got the hang of it. Found some bottle caps, some fishing hooks and a bit of loose change, but nothing really of any value, but I thought maybe I'd dig a bit anyway. What the heck, I was so antsy from being around my wife's people, and I had so much energy, and for some reason, I just felt like the spot I found was a good one for somebody wanting to hide something valuable.

After a little while, I quit for a bit and sat in the sun—it was hard work—and then I had a Fresca and a lutefisk and sauerkraut sandwich that my wife packed for me and I was thinking maybe I'd just give up and start heading back, but something kept tugging at me, like someone was pulling on my sleeve. Yeah, I know that sounds crazy, but I didn't have anything better to do anyway, and it was like I was in a movie where I was alone on a desert island in the middle of the ocean and then there was this little voice in the wind that urged me to keep digging.

I tell you though, I almost gave up. Looked like some storm clouds were coming, but they kind of blew off to the north and the rain totally missed me. I was a little nervous that I hadn't really kept track of where I was going and wasn't completely sure I could find my way back to where Gus was picking me up. Of course, I do have a pretty darn good sense of direction, I must say. My wife says I'm like a compass. She says she read that men have more metal in their nose and can tell directions better than woman. Heck, she gets lost coming home from the grocery store, so compared to her…

But like I told the other fellow earlier, I found some interesting looking rocks and then a few more, and then suddenly I hit something really solid, but it turned out that it was just another rock. I've always liked rocks and have been interested in them since I was a kid and had a rock collection, but I don't remember any of the names of the different rocks, just maybe a couple like rose quartz and pyrite. I think I would have liked to be a geologist or maybe a meteorologist—a weather man that is. Like those storm clouds—I'm pretty sure they might have been cirrus clouds or maybe cumulus come to think of it. I used to like that science stuff, but you have to make a living and heck, selling farm implements is not anything to be ashamed of.

I've made a good living over the years. Not enough to get rich of course, but the wife didn't complain. Well maybe a bit, but who could blame her. I'm not exactly the greatest catch myself, am I?

The point? Oh yes, well I was digging along and I don't know why, but I kept getting deeper and deeper and I was just about ready to give it up because I was getting awfully tired, when I noticed it.

Well, I have to say, it was quite a shock. I'm not sure my heart will ever be the same. At first I thought maybe my eyes were betraying me. There was some fabric, and I thought 'that's strange, why would anyone bury their treasure in cloth?' I always thought I'd read they used wooden chests or maybe metal boxes? And I thought maybe it was a booby trap like that Oak Island thing, but then maybe it was a flag, or maybe it was just a dump for some hobos. It kind of looked like blue jean material.

So I started poking around a bit and I thought I saw something white and hard and I said to myself, 'Glorybee, what in tarnation is this treasure after all?' And I wished the wife were with me, because she's real good at figuring out what to do. That's one of the reasons I married her, she's as solid as a rock when it comes to knowing what to do in any situation. Like that time in Bloomington, oh my. Yup, she's the one with the common sense. I'm the one with my head in the clouds half the time.

Well, yes, I suspect you would like me to describe what I saw, but I have to tell you, I have never seen anything like it, except maybe on TV or the movies, or when I took the Boy Scouts to the big museum in Chicago and we saw those mummies. Oh that was another time. Almost lost young Jimmy Wilson in the dinosaur exhibit, but for the wife again.

But that's what I am telling you. It was like it was a fossil. I could see it was bone and I thought maybe found a tyrannosaur or brontosaur bone and I'd be rich and famous, so I kneeled down and got a closer look and...

It was a skull. A human skull with long blond hair.

CHAPTER THIRTY-FIVE

"I caught him June," the caller exclaimed.

"Who?"

"That drifter that Stan Jacobson saw a few nights ago."

"Where is he now?"

"He busted into the Ferguson's summer home and slept there last night. Neighbor called it in because she knew they were in Florida this time of year. I'm holding him for you."

"I'll be right there."

Junior's anger grew as he gathered up his gear and left the office. *What was wrong with these people?* he thought. *Nothing but a pain in my side and wasting my time. Have to make an example out of them. That's what my Daddy would do.*

He had worked himself up pretty good by the time he pulled into the driveway and parked. Striding inside, he found a disheveled young man dressed in a T-shirt and ratty jeans kneeling on the floor. His hair was long and matted and he wore a long unkempt beard. Junior guessed that he was in his late twenties, although he looked much older due to the wrinkles on his sunburned face. A uniformed deputy stood over him as the man trembled. Junior tapped the young man on the side of his head.

"So where you from, Sonny?"

"I... I..."

"Didn't catch that," Junior said and tapped him a bit harder this time.

"Idaho."

"Oh ho, the land o' potatoes. So what you doing in our town?"

"Passing through."

Junior turned to the deputy. "He got a name?

"No ID on him, Sheriff."

"You got a name?" he asked the man.

"Uh... John."

"Last name?"

"Freeman."

"You always break into people's houses while you're passing through... Mr. Freeman?"

"I was cold and tired, and it didn't look like anyone else was using it. I didn't steal anything."

"You eat any of their food?"

"OK, I ate a can of soup. Sorry, I was hungry."

"Were you planning to leave any money for the Ferguson's to pay for the food you ate?"

"I... I don't have any."

"You don't have any. Do you hear that Deputy? He has no money. Well now that is a shame."

"Take him in the other room and explain to him that we really don't want people who don't have money stopping in our town and stealing from our honest citizens."

The deputy dragged the man, as he pleaded quietly, into a bedroom. Junior listened with pleasure to the thuds of fists on meat and bone followed by moans of pain that emanated from behind the door. The sheriff sat down on the couch and thumbed through an old copy of *TV Guide* for a few minutes until the pair returned, the beaten man bowed and bloodied.

"I expect Deputy Mitchell has explained the rules to you, John, and that the next time you have an urge to stop in for a visit, you will reconsider your travel plans and avoid passing through Iron County."

Junior stood up.

"I'll take it from here, Deputy. John-Boy, we're going to take a little drive over to the county line and drop you off and you can just keep on limping west. I suspect you're in a hurry to get back home to Idaho anyway, what with all those spuds waiting for you."

Junior and the deputy loaded the wounded man into the backseat of Junior's cruiser and then he drove his way leisurely through town and out along the highway. He glanced in the rear view mirror at his prisoner and softened his voice as they drove further away from the city limits.

"You know I didn't want you to leave town thinking I'm just a hard ass, John. It's just I have a thing about people who break rules and I especially don't like freeloaders. Now why didn't you just

145

stay in Idaho and pick potatoes? You've gone and put me in a bad mood and I hate it when I get a bad mood. I have stomach problems you know. It's a lot of responsibility making sure this county runs the right way and when folks like you, or should I say parasites, pests, vermin show up, well someone has to call the exterminator."

"Are we to the county line yet? My ribs feel broken." the young man spoke through bloody, swollen lips. "I think I need a hospital."

"Naw kid, you just need some rest. I know a place you can stay. Nice and warm. Kind of smells like shit. Hope you don't mind." He turned the cruiser off the highway and headed down a tree-lined back road.

"You sure. I really don't feel so good."

"Sure as shooting. I'm really a nice guy. See down this dead end road here there's an abandoned house all boarded up. The guy who built it went bankrupt and left it to me when he split town. You'll be safe here—snug as a bug."

Junior pulled the car up and parked. Pulling the vagrant out of the back seat, he pushed him forward on wobbly legs toward the house.

"They aren't going to arrest me for trespassing?" the young man asked, while spitting blood.

"Who? Arrest you? I'm the law here and nobody will bother you unless I give the say so."

"Thanks, I guess. So can I sleep in the house?"

"Oh hell, the heat's turned off, but I got something even better."

"You do?"

"Here we go. Out back here." Junior half pushed, half dragged the man along. "See that concrete sticking out there?"

"Yeah…"

"It's the entrance to a fucking bomb shelter."

"No shit?"

"Guy who built the house built it. He was rich as fuck at the time, but paranoid—whooee. Thought the government was out to get him. Filled it full of food and champagne and porn and everything you need to survive when the nukes hit. Nobody would ever find you in there and you can stay as long as you want."

146

"It's got food? You sure I won't get in trouble. Like for breaking and entering."

"Naw. Let's just unlock it and slide the top off—there you go."

"Whew, stinks like… rotting sewage?"

"I warned you, but you'll get used to it. Now just climb on down."

"Where are the lights? I don't see a ladder."

"Well I guess you better jump, huh?"

"You're joking."

He turns to try to run and spots the gun in Junior's hand.

"Bullets rarely joke, John. In fact, I really don't think they ever do."

"Why are you doing this?

"We can't have you going back home to Idaho and telling your family that we didn't show you the appropriate hospitality, now can we?

"I can't… I won't…"

Junior sighed. "Well then… guess I'll just have to give you a hand."

In a sudden burst, he rushed his bulky body forward and toppled the wounded man into the hole.

"Ohhh ughhh arrrr this is…"

"What's wrong, Mr. Freeman, aren't your accommodations up to your usual standards? Oh I forgot that you are from Idaho. Probably all outhouses where you're from and you've never seen a septic tank before."

"Oh Christ oh no please…."

"I can only imagine it is pretty bad down there—we have quite a few parties out here, and the guys are kind of pigs—lots of Mexcian food you know. Hey, dude, it's not like I don't feel for you, but you did bring this on yourself."

"No. take me to jail."

"Jail? And charge the hard working taxpayers of our fine county to feed you? It's chili night tonight. I don't think you deserve chili, do you? No, this is where you and others of your kind belong."

"You can't leave me here!"

"Don't worry, just feel around a bit son, you'll find you aren't alone in there."

147

The vagrant's screams reverberated from within the tank and dissipated in the forest air.

Struggling some with the weight, Junior slowly slid the heavy concrete lid back over the tank and locked it into place, muffling the panicked cries from within; and, feeling quite proud of himself, the Sheriff executed a perfect *en l'air* as he made his way back across the yard to his car.

CHAPTER THIRTY-SIX

The old man pulled the clattering van into the driveway and exhaled a sigh as he glanced at the silent figure slumped beside him. The woman—his wife, had fallen asleep, her face pressed against the glass. A slight strand of spittle hung from her open mouth with the other end attached to the window. A feeling of disgust momentarily filled him, but he choked it back as he sat quietly for a moment and pondered his passenger.

What happened to the little girl I loved, the one I couldn't live without. Once she burned me like a flame—her long blonde hair hanging in thick curls, her body soft and warm as he held her close on the dance floor. Now she was just a shell, a hollow husk, her body twisted and shrunken and bony, her head nearly bald save for a few gray strands and stubble.

He opened his door and stepped out, weary, with the familiar sense of dread and sadness nearly overwhelming him, but he steadied himself and opened the hatchback and lifted the wheelchair from the back. The effort nearly undid him and he had to rest for moment, his hands on his knees.

Once I was strong as an ox. He thought as he wheezed. *This is what age does—makes a mockery of us all. God is mocking us.*

He rolled the wheelchair to the passenger door and opened it carefully, reaching a hand in as he did, he pressed it against her face, ensuring that his love's head did not fall sideways.

Her neck is so brittle. If she fell just so, it would snap like a twig. Perhaps in the end, that would be more just... more humane than allowing her pain to go on? No, I can't think like that.

149

The woman opened her eyes and murmured something unintelligible.

"We're home, darling," he said comfortingly and stroked her cheek, removing the moisture from around her lips.

She attempted a painful smile. Her glassy eyes glistened with a teary gloss. He reached in to gently lift her out of the seat. It was a struggle; he felt weak, exhausted, dragged down into the depths of the earth. He needed rest. They both just needed to sleep. If only they had had children, he thought bitterly for the millionth time, someone to help him take care of her.

Turning, holding the gnarled figure in his arms, he saw the boy walking toward them out of the woods.

He's come to help us, he thought and almost had time to smile.

CHAPTER THIRTY-SEVEN

"You sure this is the place?" Lance asked.

"Yes sir, the call said to be here at 11pm."

"Go over it again, who called?"

"Some kid. He called an hour ago. Said he saw what happened to the boys. Said he'll only talk to you and not to tell anyone or involve the cops. Says he's scared of them and doesn't want to get into any trouble."

"I don't blame him. The cops around here seem like a bunch of inbred troglodytes, with that Pultz character the biggest ass of all. Did the caller say the boys were here? Are they alive? God, I hope so."

"Didn't say. He only said he needed to tell you the details face to face."

"Sounds more like a confession. You might have to beat it out of him."

"Gladly."

"He didn't care about you guys tagging along?"

"He didn't seem too happy about it at first, but he agreed when I said we wouldn't leave you alone."

Taylor and his two bodyguards walked down the dirt road and through the open gate in the wire fence and approached the entrance to the mine cautiously.

"God, this place is creepy as fuck. I'm going to call the ex," Taylor said as he pulled out his cell phone.

"The kid said not to call anyone—"

"Fuck him. Damn, it's her machine.

"Hey Sharon, this is Lance. Hey, we got a call tonight and we're following up a lead. We're at the North Star Mine. I'll let you know as soon as we're done here. The cops don't know about it yet. We have to keep it quiet for now. Shouldn't take long. I'll call back in the morning. Get some sleep."

The man hung up the phone, and, taking one last look around at the dark woods, he and the men entered the cavern entrance.

"Abandon all hope," Taylor muttered.

Their flashlights glanced off the rugged rock walls surrounding them as, stumbling over rubble, they traversed along the rusted rails and advanced deeper into the mine.

"Brrrr, damp down here ain't it?"

"Yeah and claustrophobic too." Wheeler said with a shudder. "And they say you have to be careful about fumes down in these places."

"Maybe we should skip it," suggested Powell. "Come back in the daylight."

"What's the matter, you two afraid of the dark?"

"I'm wondering if someone wasn't just pulling our leg."

"Well the kid sounded sincere. He also sounded scared for his life."

"Maybe they got to him first. Hello! Is anybody here?" Taylor called out, his voice echoing away into the distance.

"I say we turn around and go home, Boss."

Suddenly from a distant place further down the passageway, a faint tapping could be heard.

"Shhh...You hear that?" Taylor whispered.

"Kid, is that you?" Powell called out and reached for his pistol.

"Cole, are you there? Is that you, Cole?" Taylor shouted frantically.

The response was silence for a long moment, while the men held their breath and stood still, before the faint tapping recommenced.

"It's coming from down there," Powell said and pointed down the dark corridor that veered off to the right.

Taylor rushed forward down the spur, flashlight in hand, his men following rapidly as they pressed on into the cave, the jagged walls emitting a more pronounced chill as they moved deeper— calling out as they went.

"Hello, hello!"

"Over there," Powell shouted and pointed down a side passage. As they hurried down the drift, they finally spotted what appeared to be a light coming from somewhere near the end of the path.

"Looks like they had a cave-in," Wheeler muttered as they stepped over piles of rubble to where there was an opening in the wall.

Peering into the entrance to the chamber they saw a flashlight perched on a boulder and a boy's jacket draped over what appeared to be a small body.

"Christ!"

The men clambered in through the small opening and rushed across the small room

"Cole!"

"Kid. Hey Kid!"

They reached the jacket and pulled it off to reveal a pile of rubble and dirt mounded into a vague body shape. Frantically they began to search the corners of the chamber, finding it empty.

"Shit, do you think—?"

Before they could retreat, an explosive blast suddenly reverberated through the room, shaking the ground beneath them. The men fell down and a rain of rocks and debris came sliding down, nearly sealing the hole, except for a small opening less than a foot across. As they rushed back to what was left of the opening they saw a familiar face grinning at them through the dust.

"You!" Wheeler cried out.

"What is this all about, Pultz?" demanded Taylor, brushing the dust off his suit.

"Nothing personal fellas, but I have to tidy things up a bit. I'm bucking to be Sheriff soon, as you know, and I can't have any skeletons hanging around in my closet now can I?"

"You set this up?"

"I am sadly unaware of the details and can only surmise you and your detectives here must have followed a lead and entered this dangerous mine in search of those poor lost boys. Well-intentioned, no doubt, but ultimately a very bad idea. You see that's why we have a fence and no trespassing signs posted outside—these darn rockslides can happen at any time."

"There weren't any signs and the fence was open," Powell protested.

"Gosh, were the signs down? We better put them back up right away. And, you must be mistaken, the gate was locked tight. We found where you cut through the fence."

Wheeler raised his gun.

"Uh uh, I wouldn't do that. Might cause another rockslide," Junior said with a snicker.

"What do you want? Money?"

"Hmmm… money, wealth, fame… what do I want? Oh you big city sophisticates, don't you know that us small town bumpkins don't need anything? We're happy with our place in life. We got stars and trees and the wind and the snow and heck, we don't need any caviar or champagne to make us happy. Nope, I figure I got everything I need right now."

"This isn't some cheap novel. You can't just kill people and get away with it."

"Well, it is true that I don't know much about novels, per se', I tend to read mostly non-fiction, myself—"

"Pultz!"

"But I've seen a movie or two and have a bit of an idea about how this might play out. I can only imagine how terrible it would be to be trapped in this godforsaken place hour after hour, the oxygen getting used up little by little. Flashlights burning out, alone in the dark, cold and hungry. Hey, better draw straws to see who gets eaten first. I'll bet it's Mr. Powell there, unless you prefer dark meat. Ha!"

"You're insane. And you won't get away with it. I called Sharon—"

"And left a message. Yes, I know. Naughty, naughty—you weren't supposed to contact anyone, were you? But that's OK, I anticipated your duplicity and ensured that Sharon would be asleep when you called. Deep asleep, you might say. Poor girl should never mix sleeping pills with alcohol you know. So sorry about your message, I suspect it must have been erased by now."

"No… Sharon!" Taylor gasped.

"What do you care? You dumped her for a younger model or was it two, several years ago. What's the phrase—traded a forty for two twenties?"

"Why you, I never…"

"We'll get out, Pultz, and when we do—"

"Did you bring shovels? No? A jackhammer perhaps, or possibly some explosives? Well then, that is unfortunate. But you do have a couple of strapping men with you, Taylor, and I am quite sure you all will work tirelessly to remove the rocks and debris by hand in your heroic, yet ultimately futile bid for safety. Maybe if you say your prayers, you can roll away the stone and emerge resurrected, but I don't think so. No, I'm afraid all your efforts will be in vain. In vein, get it? You're trapped in a mine. Oh well, I thought it was funny."

He turned away and called out, "Gary!"

The sudden roar of an engine starting up was heard in the distance and got louder as headlights from a vehicle driving slowly down the path appeared.

"What the hell—?"

"Oh, forgive my rudeness. Let me introduce you to my friend Gary. Gary here owns this mine. He's a very good friend of mine. He owes me a favor or two. Likes to help me out when he can, and he's quite happy to help me finish up this job, aren't ya' Gar?"

"For the love of God, Pultz!" Taylor pleaded as the roar grew louder, as a bobcat appeared, moving over the debris on heavy treads.

"Oh, come on, you can call me Junior. We're friends now aren't we, Lance?"

"Pultz... Junior, before you go... just tell me. Are the boys still alive?"

Junior pondered how to answer the question before responding.

"Don't you know Lance, people are always alive if you keep them alive in your heart. Yeah, in hindsight, I think that's probably what you should have done—kept them alive in your heart. Well, goodbye."

Junior retreated. Wheeler and Powell fired their pistols as the excavator covered the hole with dirt and rock. One of the bullets ricocheted off the metal blade hitting Powell who screamed in pain, as Taylor cried out with one last plea, "Junior!" before his voice was muffled forever.

Junior patted Gary on the back as he passed by the bobcat operator, and continued on, chuckling to himself *look who's got the power now*, as he made his way back out of the depths of the pit.

CHAPTER THIRTY-EIGHT

"I remember now."

"What do you remember?"

"That day. The day I…"

"Go on."

"Now I say I remember, but we both know I never really forgot. How could you forget something like that?"

"You were knocked unconscious. That your memory is hazy would only be expected."

"Yeah, hazy is the word. But through the shadows, I could see him looming over me and…"

"Yes?"

"He was gonna stomp me… stomp me to death. And I saw myself, lying dead and bleeding in the parking lot and then something just took hold of me—"

"Adrenaline?"

"I wanted to live. I didn't want to die."

"It's only natural."

"But my body just kind of leapt up by itself. It hurt like hell, my ribs… and I could hardly see through the blood gushing from my nose but then I… I…"

"Then what happened? Please finish the story."

"I reached under my jacket and pulled out the bottle…"

"A bottle of Everclear." She checked her notes. "Where did you get that?"

"She gave it to me."

"She?"

"Betty, Ches' wife. She was just being nice. She knew we were just looking to catch a buzz and—"

"Were you involved in a… relationship with Mrs. Jensen?"

"What? Oh hell no. We flirted around a bit, but she was an old lady."

"It says here she was only thirty-four—maybe looks a bit older than her age, but she was hardly an old crone."

"I admit she wasn't terrible looking, but still way too old for me. I don't go for older women… well maybe in your case."

"Did Chester think you were involved with his wife?"

"What? Yeah I guess he must've thought so, but that's just crazy talk. He was just nuts and out of his head about the beer. And he always was crazy jealous of her too, but who knows where he got the idea that I was the one sleeping with her? I just know that he was going to kill me."

"You truly believed he was going to kill you."

"I sure did."

"He was a very large man and trained in martial arts."

"They said he was a kick boxer, but got his brains beat in. Still, he was pretty tough and mean."

"So how did it… end?"

"You know. I popped him."

"Popped him"

"Yeah, I wasn't even thinking. It was like I was on automatic pilot or something and I just went off and wailed on him."

"You struck him with the bottle how many times?"

"Just the once. Thought I heard his skull crunch when the glass broke and then it all went black."

"You didn't keep hitting him?"

"I don't think so."

"His head was quite damaged for it being only one blow."

157

"I hit him with all I had and that's all I remember, I swear. I think they said I passed out at that point."

The psychologist put down the folder and note pad and sat forward.

"Well Jeremy, now don't you see? You were just a boy, perhaps a troubled boy, but one who found himself in a dangerous situation facing a large adult man with a violent temper and reacted the only way you could, to survive. Forgive yourself. You aren't guilty of anything wrong, Jeremy, except trying to live. You are a survivor and because you chose to survive, you now have the opportunity to leave the broken boy and these terrible memories behind when you leave this facility and create yourself a new future—one filled with hope and promise."

"It was over money—"

"No Jeremy, it wasn't."

"I could've let him keep the money. I didn't have to show the guys."

"Forgive yourself, Jeremy. You have to learn to forgive yourself for what you did."

"I could have hit him with my fist, I could have played dead."

"And you might be dead now instead of him."

"I could have hit him with less force. I could have hit him an inch or two lower and maybe knocked him out instead of killing—"

"No, you are wrong; it was self-defense. Don't you see? You had no choice then. You just didn't… But now you do. You just have to develop the self-discipline necessary to avoid falling back into your old habits and routines when you return home."

"You don't have to worry about that, Doctor."

"Why is that, Jeremy?"

"Because I am never going back to Crystal Falls."

CHAPTER THIRTY-NINE

All eyes were on Junior as his pear-shaped body skipped lightly to the front of the room, and looked out humbly with his small, piggish eyes gleaming, upon the friendly faces that looked back at him with admiration. The Sheriff patted him on the back and whispered "Congratulations, June – you'll make a great Sheriff after I retire in a few years." Sid and Junior moved to the side as the mayor stepped forward to the podium.

As the mayor began his narration, Junior leaned over and whispered to his boss, "Was gonna talk to you about that, Sid. I've been thinking—why put it off? In fact, I was thinking you ought to announce your retirement and my promotion to Sheriff today while we are all gathered together,"

"What?" the Sheriff looked startled. Junior smiled.

"It's just this, Sid. You know, I've been thinking this through for a while now, and well, you probably got enough saved up by now, and you'll get a pretty nice pension, and heck you can move down south and not have to shovel snow and can be remembered fondly by the people of the town, or... they could all learn about your propensity for kiddie porn and those 'sleepovers' with the little boys of the Junior Rangers that your wife doesn't seem to know about."

"I...I... !" the Sheriff sputtered.

"It's Ok Sid, I understand." Junior patted the Sheriff on his back. "Life is a weird ride and everybody's got their own hoedown to attend. I'm not here to judge. But how would Nancy take the news?"

Junior winked and waved to Sid's wife as he spoke quietly and menacingly into Sid's ear.

"I expect it would just about break her to pieces," Junior continued. "And you know how the people talk in this town. Hell, we'd never hear the end of it. Just Stan Jacobson alone with his big mouth and pretty soon it's national news. Maybe I could even share a photo in the papers of you bent over helping a boy tie his shoes, except he wasn't wearing any shoes and—come to think of it, neither were you—because you were both in the shower."

Sid sputtered, red-faced. "How—?"

"You always kidded me for my reading, but I'm learning all sorts of skills from it. Lately, I've been teaching myself photography. Fascinating subject—f-stops, apertures, telephoto lenses—"

"What the hell do you want, you little shit?"

"Come on Sid, you know what I want. Now's your chance to walk away with what's left of your pride and no one's the wiser. Heck it ain't like they don't have little boys just about anywhere you want to go—except, maybe, prison. But, heck, I'm sure they'd make you feel real welcome there, don't ya' think, 'Short Eyes'?"

"You gotta give me some time—"

"Time for you to weasel out of it somehow? To put a bullet in my back? No, time is of the essence and I think now is as good a time as any, don't you? I've been patient long enough. The time is now. Otherwise I enter my latest photo studies into the big competition at the County Fair. I'll just bet they give me the big purple ribbon this year for sure."

"Alright, alright, but you are one evil sonofabitch, you know that."

"Now now, you don't you be talking about my mother that way, you hear," Junior waved to his mom in the crowd and smiled as he threatened his boss. "I won't have you do that. I won't. She's as good an angel as there ever was on earth, and you are just going to be a good boy and just step right up and make this the happiest day she has ever had. Let's go now, Sid."

As the mayor finished his speech and the crowd applauded, the sheriff approached the podium, appearing only slightly flustered and quickly composed himself. "Thank you, Mr. Mayor for your opening remarks. Now I will award Deputy Pultz with this commendation from the Governor himself for the excellent work he did in discovering the bodies of the missing Taylor boy and his friend and bringing them home so their families could lay them to rest."

160

Sharon Taylor stood to one side in the front row, and with tears streaming down her face, mouthed *thank you* to Junior.

"And just how did our... 'hero' find the boys? Just good old fashioned police work, Just like his daddy Roy, Sr. before him, the apple obviously doesn't fall far from the tree—and Mrs. Pultz, you have raised yourself a fine and upstanding young man with a very bright future ahead."

Although she really could not fully hear the words or completely understand the meaning of the ceremony, Junior's mother beamed with pride anyway, knowing her boy was performing in front of people again and wishing in her heart that he would break out in song.

"It was only through an amazing act of deduction," the Sheriff continued, "that Roy here was able to determine that the boys must have been hot-rodding out of town after the incident at the gas station and may have misjudged a turn at an unsafe rate of speed, causing the Camaro to fly off the road, through a dense thicket of trees and into a pond, where the car sank and the battered and unconscious boys were unfortunately drowned.

"Now the bodies, I am sorry to report were decomposed to such a state that the coroner is unable to determine an exact cause of death, but the important thing is Deputy Pultz took the initiative and never gave up in his relentless search for justice. If we had only known that the boys were here under our noses the whole time... I mean, I myself have taken several of the Junior Rangers swimming in that very pond and—"

Sid suddenly began choking and had to swallow a mouthful of water before continuing on.

"The sad irony that the boys were found shortly after we found his father Lance Taylor and his men deceased in the old North Star Mine where the desperate father was apparently searching for the lost boys and got trapped by a cave-in is truly heartbreaking. And let me just add to let that be a lesson to amateurs and the public in general – crime is hard and dangerous work and you should leave the solving of such matters and of course, crimes, to the true professionals."

Sid reached into his pocket and pulled out a gaudy, gold metallic badge with red, white and blue ribbons.

161

"Now the National Sheriff's Association has provided June…
er Roy here with a medal that I will now pin on him as apt
recompense for his valor, integrity and honor."

As he pinned the medal roughly to Junior's chest, the sheriff
whispered "I hope you rot in hell."

"You'll be there before me, let me know how you like it. Better
yet, take a picture and send it to me," Junior responded cheerfully.

"Fuck off," the sheriff said with a smile.

Sid turned back to the crowd and gestured.

"And now Sharon Taylor has generously paid the reward
offered by her husband…"

She hands a check to Junior. "Thank you so much, for bringing
our Cole home to us."

Junior bowed his head and blushed as she handed him a check
and kissed his cheek. Then with tears on her face, she returned to
the crowded audience to lead the applause. Junior assumed an
impressive air of humility as he raised the check up and
acknowledged the cheering crowd before beginning his address.

"I am honored and humbled by the outpouring of support
today. I only wish I would have seen Cole Taylor and his friend
and could have stopped the boys before their accident, but I am
thankful to the Lord God above that I was able to find the boys and
bring them home at last. And while I could certainly use a raise,
you hear me Sid…?"

The crowd laughed loudly as Junior continued. "…You know
that I simply cannot in good conscience accept this payment, as I
was only doing my job, and accepting these funds could potentially
impinge upon the propriety and ethics of my office, which I
cherish and hold dear to the memory of my late father."

The crowd hushed as Junior paused.

"I will however," he continued "donate these funds to the
middle school in order to renovate the playground, which I will
insist be named in Cole Taylor's honor."

The crowd gasped and then clapped vigorously.

"Oh thank you," sobbed Sharon. "What a beautiful thought."

Junior held up his hand to quiet the applause.

"And any funds left over will be deposited to the Sheriff's
Widows and Orphans Fund to provide support to family members
of those brave officers killed in the line of duty."

A nearly deafening roar of appreciation burst forth from the crowd and Junior was awarded with a standing ovation and vociferous cheering, which Sid stepped in hurriedly to break up.

"Well that just about concludes this gathering," the Sheriff announced gruffly. "There are refreshments provided by the Ladies Auxiliary in the room next door that we hope you will help yourself to—"

Junior nudged Sid, who reluctantly continued.

"But before you go… As long as we are in the announcing mood, I have one more to make…"

Junior blew a kiss at his mother as he was awarded the throne.

CHAPTER FORTY

The young kids ran screaming through the grassy back yard—the pint-sized little boy chasing the slightly taller girl while dangling a plastic snake in her face whenever she stopped running, causing the girl to squeal in mock fright. Their young mother stepped out onto the porch and told them to be quiet, and they argued good-naturedly for a moment, before she retreated back into the interior of the trailer. Seemingly undisturbed by his mother's half-hearted attempt at discipline, the boy sank to the ground and began building fortifications in the dirt for his armies of plastic soldiers, preparing for the impending battle to save humanity against the menace of the giant snake. The girl, meanwhile, climbed onto a swing and rocked herself back and forth, softly singing to herself a raucous radio song made popular by a heavily made-up entertainer about an especially proficient lover—without, of course, having even the vaguest notion of understanding the actual meaning of the words she mouthed.

The boy in the woods watched them from his vantage point on the hill, silently calculating the situation. It seemed like the right move. He had been watching the home for hours and there was no sign of a father—no male presence at all: no pickup truck in the driveway; no canoe in the back yard. He'd seen no one else; the woman and her children appeared to be alone. The woman somewhat reminded him of his own mother, always trying to stop the boy from having fun. He would have no problem ridding the world of another bossy bitch. And the children... well children were easy; they do as they're told. Like he used to.

He scanned his surroundings in all directions. A house down the heavily forested street reeked of testosterone, with trucks, motorcycles, and ATVs parked everywhere; while another trailer closer by, had a yard patrolled by a pair of menacing pit bulls. He was sure he made the right choice with this trailer. He would have to be quiet, but he knew he could pull it off without raising the alarm.

He checked the perimeter again and this time noticed a ramshackle shack behind a mass of overgrown vegetation at the far end of the dirt lane that appeared to be abandoned—with its broken windows boarded up, a derelict and rusted Quonset hut behind it and no obvious signs of life. Not a bad place to hide, but he was hungry and he doubted there would be any food in that dump. So that left...

The young mother called the children in to dinner. The boy in the woods could just make out the odor of what he recognized as hot dogs and mac-n-cheese and hoped they would leave enough for him. His stomach grumbled and he anxiously watched the horizon.

The sun would be down soon.

CHAPTER FORTY-ONE

And so I saw the wicked buried, who had come and gone from the place of the holy, and they were forgotten in the city where they had so done: this is also vanity.

They've finally found him. It is all over the news. Jesse Ray's body has been found on the island where I killed and buried him so many years ago.

For God giveth to a man that is good in his sight wisdom, and knowledge, and joy: but to the sinner he giveth travail, to gather and to heap up, that he may give to him that is good before God. This also is vanity and vexation of spirit.

Soon they will put the evidence together and I will be found out and brought to earthly justice. As if I have not suffered enough for my sins.

Wilt thou break a leaf driven to and fro? and wilt thou pursue the dry stubble?
Thou puttest my feet also in the stocks, and lookest narrowly unto all my paths; thou settest a print upon the heels of my feet.

But they don't know what I know. That body that they found is not Jesse Ray, but merely an empty shell. Jesse is still here and he remains with me here in my room. He stands over me constantly mocking me with hurt and angry eyes; and I know he will never leave this place until I do.

Though a sinner do evil an hundred times, and his days be prolonged, yet surely I know that it shall be well with them that fear God, which fear before him

By mercy and truth iniquity is purged: and by the fear of the Lord men depart from evil.

Soon my secret will be revealed and the heavy weight that presses down on me will be lifted. But my joy at the thought is burdened with dread, for although my remaining earthly stay may well be brief, it is said that Hell is for eternity. Or will forgiveness be my gift at last?

Behold, happy is the man whom God correcteth: therefore despise not thou the chastening of the Almighty:
For he maketh sore, and bindeth up: he woundeth, and his hands make whole.

CHAPTER FORTY-TWO

Junior burst through the front door and found his wife asleep on the couch with the television on—the coffee table next to her strewn with beer bottles and an overflowing ashtray. He shut off the TV and angrily nudged her awake.

"Get up, damn it."

"Wha... what time is it?" She replied sleepily, yawning and stretching as she awoke and sat up.

"It's 3:30 in the afternoon. Thanks for coming to my big event, Jenny."

"Oh shit. Yeah sorry." she said dully and blinked her eyes. "I wasn't feeling well and took some medicine. Must have knocked me out."

"Yeah, well you really embarrassed me...again."

"So what? Are you going to tell your mother on me? She was there no doubt."

"Of course she was there, it was the most important day of my life."

"Ha,"Jenny snorted.

"My wife should have been there and my son too."

"Stepson, and I think we'll both pass on attending any more of your community outreach, Officer Friendly."

"Fuck you! See this medal and these framed awards they gave me. I'm a hero." He threw the medal and awards on the couch next to her in exasperation. She glanced at them out of the corner of her eye and reached for the remote to turn the TV back on.

Junior grabbed it out of her hand, and snapped, "And why the fuck don't you clean up around here and get yourself together— you look like shit and you're getting fat AGAIN."

"Talk about the pot calling the kettle black," she sneered and lit a cigarette. "So you found some dead kids in a ditch, big deal."

"A pond—and their families were quite grateful."

"No doubt. But I gotta ask you—how did they get there in the first place, Junior?" She eyed him suspiciously. "You probably put them there, didn't you? Yeah, that sounds about right. You're a real tough guy when it comes to women and children."

"You better shut up before you go too far, Jenny. You don't know what you're talking about."

"Sure I don't. So they gave you a medal and a plaque. Whoopdeedoo." Shakily, she picked up a half empty beer bottle and took a swig, nearly knocking over the ashtray with her spastic movement.

Junior grabbed her by the wrist.

"You stupid bitch, are you using again?"

She glared at him with piercing eyes.

"I thought I locked your stash up," he roared. "You must have some in your doll room. I'm going to—"

"You will NOT go in there," she hissed. "That is my room. My space. I've told you that if you ever go in that room, you know that I will leave you."

"Yeah right." Junior sneered, but the threat had shaken him and he softened his tone. "Where could you go?"

"Who knows?" she said and took a drag. "Maybe I'd go to Paris. Or maybe… Fargo. I could stay with my cousin, Jean."

"Right. You do that. Just go on off to Fargo. Why not Las Vegas or Tallahassee, or Hollywood even? You already must think you're a big time star what with all the scenes you are always making. You know I am tired of making excuses for you. I had to tell everyone you were sick… again. They said I should send you to the Mayo Clinic to find out what's wrong."

"Might be fun," she snarled and took a big drink from the open beer on the coffee table. "Just think what the townspeople would think. deputy's wife on drugs, and where do you suppose she got them?"

"Sheriff," Junior corrected her.

"What?"

"That's right. You heard what I said. That's my other big news. Ol' Sid made it official, he's retiring and moving south and put me in charge."

"He can't do that," she said and stubbed out her cigarette in the ashtray.

"Sure he can."

"You have to be elected."

"OK, I'm only the acting Sheriff for now, but when we have the next election, I will win. The people love me. I'm a hero."

"Sid wasn't planning on retiring any time soon. What the hell did you do?" She lit another cigarette and glared at him.

"Nothing much, just a little minor persuasion. You know how much he loves fishing and how cold it gets here in the winter and—heck, why wait until you can't enjoy life before you leave the daily grind. He's got enough money squirreled away, and he's done enough for this town and can leave while he's on top and let a younger man take his place—like me."

She took a long drag and addressed him with a sneer on her face.

"Hmm, so you did it at last. Made your dear old daddy proud. Too bad he's dead and can't see just how much you've taken after him. Guess you're the big man now, huh Junior?"

"Yup. I am."

"Well la de da."

"You have to quit the drugs Jenny."

"Why do you care? You're the one selling the shit."

"It's killing you."

"Let it be, Junior," she threatened and drained the beer bottle and smacked it back on the coffee table. "It's the only reason I stay with you." Reaching out quickly, she grabbed the remote out of Junior hands, and, turning on the TV, she lay back down on the couch as she dismissed him.

CHAPTER FORTY-THREE

I find myself walking alone in a damp dark forest. I can feel my feet sink in the wet muddy ground as I struggle to make my way forward through the heavy brush. Branches and thick vegetation scratch my face and hands as I force my way through the densely entwined black thicket. Above, the moon is mostly hidden by clouds and I can barely find my path in the enveloping darkness.

Far in the distance I hear an owl cry. I try to follow the sound, tripping and stumbling over rough terrain and up and over a rocky rise and into an open hollow.

Mother, I'm going to find you. Not like you found me, that time. You let me down. You didn't find me when I needed you. But I swear that I am going to find you.

I enter an opening ringed by trees. There is a mound of dirt in the center of the clearing. The moonlight shines down on it giving it the appearance of an altar—like something those ancient people would build to worship their dark gods. The owl's cry intensifies and becomes that of a woman screaming, crying out in pain and fear.

The voice is muffled; it comes from below the dirt. I recognize it: it is my mother's voice.

I kneel and begin to dig frantically with my hands. The more I unearth, the deeper the grave seems, until at last I strike a wooden plank. The voice is louder now; it is shouting in my ears. I hear pounding from within the box—scratching, clawing.

I uncover the lid and strain with all my strength to force open the coffin. It opens slowly, painfully, with great difficulty. I am crying out loud all the time: "I'm here. I'll save you, Mom. I love you."

Pulling the wooden top back at last, I stare deep into the blackness of the tomb and see a face emerge from its depths.

It is my own.

I awake with a scream to find Katy's arms comforting me.

CHAPTER FORTY-FOUR

"Iron County has a sickness. There is a blackness, an evil hanging over this county. You all know it in your hearts." Ethan Andrews stood on the stage at the high school and looked out over the assembled crowd as he spoke into the handheld microphone. Scanning the gathering, he searched the audience for Pastor Carlsson and was disappointed not to see his old friend in attendance. The absence of his most faithful supporter threw him for a moment, and he realized that he hadn't seen the pastor since his wife had had lunch with the pastor yesterday while Ethan was getting his hair cut. He remembered Mary had mentioned something in her quiet mousy voice about the pastor getting sick, but Ethan had been too busy to worry about it at the time as he was busy preparing his speech, and he had glossed it over at the time, hoping his trusted advisor would get over whatever was ailing him in time to attend his triumphant defeat over the fat man.

The former CIA agent took a breath and composed himself. He took pride in his unruffled demeanor and forged ahead confidently with his beautifully written speech.

"But it doesn't have to be this way. This is lovely town, surrounded by wonderful lakes, rivers and forests. People would want to live here for its beauty and peaceful nature—for its hiking and rafting and hunting and fishing, and to raise their children, if only it was safe and... uncorrupted." Several people in the crowd nodded their heads in agreement.

"Change is sometimes hard, but it is inevitable if one wants to succeed. We need to change this place—you know it and I know it—and I am asking you to trust me with helping to lead this change. Once I am elected, we will be able to welcome new people into the town, and bring back industry, jobs and opportunities for our young people so they don't have to move away or get into trouble, because idle hands are the devil's hands as we all know. I know I am a newcomer, an outsider, but in the short time we've lived here, my wife and I have come to love the folks we have met here and come to understand that they deeply want change, they need change to breath the fresh air again—to bring the town of Crystal Falls back to life again."

A burst of applause interrupted his delivery. Andrews took a drink of water and winked confidently at his wife standing in the wings before continuing.

"Now I am sure Sheriff Pultz loves this town too," Andrews said with a smirk, as Junior scowled at him from his seat on the stage. The Sheriff looked uneasy, pale and disheveled—with his stained uniform too tight on his pudgy body. "And I come not bury the Sheriff, but to praise him. He has done his time and served this town well—to the best of his… abilities for many, many years…"

Snickers erupted in the crowd as the man extended his oratory. "As his father did before him…"

This comment elicited a smattering of outright guffaws from the audience as they recalled the legacy of the corrupt former sheriff who infamously died in bed with a cheap hooker.

"But perhaps," Ethan went on, "it has come time to make a change—to bring new ideas, new energy and development money —and with it, the hope needed to take this town into the future." Raucous applause filled the gymnasium. Junior slid even lower in his seat.

"But it has to be a safe place for that to happen. Is Iron County safe now? I've heard the terrible stories of all the strange disappearances and unsolved murders that have occurred in the past. Why only today, I turned on my television to find out that a body has been discovered buried out on an island in the Michigamme Reservoir."

Junior's eyes opened wide and he goggled upon hearing the news.

"How can I make difference? Well, in my 30 years in the CIA, I worked with the latest in surveillance equipment, military and law enforcement technologies and intensive interrogation techniques. I infiltrated terrorist organizations and hostile foreign governments to help protect the freedoms we enjoy in this greatest nation on God's own Earth."

More applause interrupted the speech and Ethan took a drink of water before proceeding. "Put your trust in me and I promise to bring law and order to Iron County. I mean, I faced down the Red Chinese and the Viet Cong in the Far East; I fought the mass killer Almed Al-Ahdami in Tunisia and put his plan to kill Americans with a dirty bomb out of operation permanently. I have to ask you, do you think a little kid with a popgun could get away with murdering people with me in charge—?"

Junior leapt out of his seat and began shouting into his microphone in a slurred voice that made it clear that he had been drinking.

"Big deal. Real big deal," he barked, unsuccessfully trying to prevent the bursts of piercing feedback that emitted from the sound system, causing many in the audience to cringe and cover their ears. "So you blew up some rag head in the desert with a missile from 200 miles away. Is that the best you can do? Push a button. What else did you do—waterboard a half-dead, skinny, midget tied to a chair? Real tough guy, aren't you?"

Some in the audience laughed as Junior paced the floor in a rage, bellowing. "You don't know nothing about Iron County. You don't know about us at all. 'Round here, we don't push buttons on some fancy computer—we get our asses up and out from behind a desk and hunt 'em down. We get the dogs and put on our boots we go marching through the mud and the rain and the sludge and the brush until we get our man. And we will get him. He may be only a kid, but he's a Crystal Falls kid and probably a hell of lot tougher than your 'terrorist'—who was probably just a rug merchant in the wrong caravan anyway. Did the missile kill his wife and kids too? Maybe even some friends or even just people just happened to be in the neighborhood? Why don't you tell us about that, City Boy?"

Andrews glared, but he remained silent as Junior ranted. He had to keep his cool. Things were proceeding as planned. He knew the sheriff was making an ass of himself. He just had to work it to his advantage when the time came.

"You don't know what it's like to live here," Junior rambled on. "We may be old-fashioned, but that's the way we like it. Sure things aren't perfect, but what are you going to bring to the table, huh?—a quicker and more efficient way to go to hell? Maybe we don't want your 'developments' Did you ever think of that?"

His ire raised, the crimson-cheeked sheriff shouted into the squealing microphone: "You aren't one of us. You stand there so self-satisfied, winking and smirking at the 'yokels.' You with your hipster suit and your brand new cowboy boots that ain't even got a turd on 'em yet; with your hyped-up war stories and Ivy-league manners; your perfect white bread life and family right out of a Penney's catalog; your perfect teeth and your perfect wife and—"

"And where is your wife, Sheriff?" Andrews interjected with perfect timing—jubilantly perceiving that he had put Junior into checkmate and that certain victory was his at last.

The people in the audience gasped and held their breath as Junior's face turned red, his body tensed, and in an instant the Sheriff lunged himself wildly like an animal across the stage and towards his rival. Andrews was completely taken aback by the quickness and sudden ferocity of the reaction of the fat man and, too late, attempted to use his judo prowess to fling the Sheriff's bulky body overhead. Instead, the fat man landed with a thud on top of the CIA man and began pummeling him in the face with both fists. Shocked townspeople rushed onstage to pull Junior off, his opponent, who—in a moment of self-preservation managed to deliver a well-placed karate chop to the throat of the sheriff. Junior's eyes rolled back, he grabbed his throat and, choking, fell in a heap on top of the flailing man, as a riot of laughter, shouts and utter pandemonium broke out in the auditorium.

CHAPTER FORTY-FIVE

Hold me.

I feel my life slipping away.

I feel your arms around me.

It's been so long since you held me tightly in the dark.

Do you remember when you first told me you loved me, Jesse?
Do you?

That day, the three of us were driving to the quarry to go swimming. You and I in the back seat and poor Preacher behind the wheel as always.
Watching us in the rear view mirror, like he always did, as you kissed me and I kissed you back. Our lips merging into honey. I could have kissed you forever.

And I whispered *I love you.*
And you whispered *I love you* back.

Your hands on my body. Your breath on my neck and ear. Your soul and mine combining…

Until Preacher took you away! And I can never forgive him for that despite the awful price he paid.

But now I feel you with me again, Jesse. I'm no longer alone. And soon we can be together again.

Forever.

CHAPTER FORTY-SIX

The sheriff's cruiser was parked behind a thicket on the back road in the usual place. Kurt and Donald pulled in, parked their car and got out slowly. Chester's pickup was already there and two men were standing in the shadows talking as the latecomers approached.

"You gonna fix that broken taillight or am I going to have to bust you myself?" Junior snarled at Kurt, who shrugged.

"It's daytime, how'd you know it's still out?"

"You've still got the duct tape and wires hanging out, you moron."

"I'll get to it. I haven't made it to the auto parts store yet."

"You said that last week. I need you two to run down to Green Bay and pick up some goodies and I am not chancing you getting pulled over."

"I'll fix it today."

"You'll fix it now! You need to be on the road in an hour." He handed the nervous man a piece of paper. "Here are the instructions."

Kurt nodded. Donald piped up, motioning toward Chester, who was standing in the shadows several feet away, sulkily smoking a cigarette: "Is the big guy goin' us?"

"Not this time."

"Too bad, he is one scary dude. Nice to have around when the creeps get uptight. Not much of a conversationalist though."

"Fuck off and die," Chester snapped from the woods,

179

Whoa Ches, I was just joking. Lighten up, pal."

The big man just snarled and stomped several feet away to where he continued to smoke and pace around angrily.

Kurt lowered his voice. "What's buggin' the gorilla?"

"Not really your concern, but apparently someone just told him his wife is cheating on him," Junior said quietly.

Donald whistled. "Christ, that's a tough one."

"I knew he should've never married that slut," sniffed Kurt.

"Hey, hey! He's standing right over there you idiot."

"I know, but damn…"

"Well she is alone at the bar all the time and she's not a bad piece. Probably every guy who goes in there hits on her."

"Even you… and me, come to think of it."

"Well with Chester always off hunting and fishing and running around doing stuff for you, Junior, you can't really blame her for wanting to have a little fun."

"I guess not," Junior said with a slight smile.

"So what's he going to do when he catches them?"

"He'll probably murder the bastard, maybe both of them."

"You saw what he did to her last month didn't ya?"

Kurt laughed. "You couldn't miss that shiner."

"Guess I'm glad he isn't riding with us this trip. He's a powder keg on a good day; he might go off over a mosquito bite in this state of mind."

"Well, he is a little upset right now," Junior prudently advised, "and as such, I would strongly suggest you boys get a move on out of here soon."

"You think he might blow?"

"Probably, because, well, you see, what's even worse," Junior whispered confidentially, "is the guy his wife is sleeping with is a high school kid."

The men snickered into their hands—trying not to let Chester hear them. "Oh shit, that is the worst. I can't fucking believe it. Shit, shit, shit…"

"Yeah, ain't that the shit? But you guys gotta keep it quiet, right?"

"Yeah, yeah, wow, that is fucked. So Junior, I gotta ask, how did the bull moose react when he found out?"

"Don't know, but I am about to tell him."

CHAPTER FORTY-SEVEN

The blackness spread like thick lacquer over the world as the sun slid behind the hills. The boy in the woods yawned and stood up and stretched. Picking up his rifle, he stepped stealthily down the embankment toward the trailer.

Suddenly, he heard a cough in the night and froze, hiding his body behind a tree from the direction of the sound. Peering through the darkness, he searched for the source of the sound, before zeroing in on the empty shack.

Standing in front of the abandoned cabin was an old man with an unkempt white beard and greasy white hair tied in a ratty ponytail. Dressed in a filthy white t-shirt and tattered grimy overalls, the old man watched the moon and stars in the night sky as he finished his cigarette. *So, it wasn't abandoned after all*. the boy thought as he stood still, wondering if he had been spotted. The man gave no indication and seemed unaware of the boy's presence, but… how could he be sure. The smoker coughed again and bent over and spat on the ground before turning and, limping heavily, retreated on weak legs around to the back of the hovel. The boy was suddenly aware of smoke and the appealing smell of meat charring on a grill wafting from that area. His strategy was immediately changed by the introduction of this new information, and he veered down the slope, making his way cautiously toward the boarded up house.

Around the back, a single shot took the unsuspecting man down without any trouble. It was possible that the shot may have been heard, but around here with all the hunters, there wouldn't be anything unusual about it: the boy doubted it would be reported. He finished cooking the venison on the grill and stepped inside to eat and to sit down and try to escape from the mosquitos that had bedeviled him all day.

Boxes of trash piled up everywhere made it difficult to walk through the kitchen, where the counters were stacked high with dirty pots and pans, oily motorcycle parts, newspapers and other refuse. Flies swarmed nearly every surface, including the sparse bones of what appeared to be a picked over wild turkey carcass. Based on the items thrown in the sink, it did not appear to be in use and a search of the non-working refrigerator revealed nothing but mold. Jars of amber liquid were stacked in a cupboard along with a few dusty cans of beans and vegetables. The boy opened one and took a sniff. Phew... moonshine. The boy gagged and put it back.

In the living room, he clicked on the dust-covered television and, after clearing piles of unwashed laundry and old motorcycle and girlie magazines off of the stained and lumpy couch, sat down to relax. He was disappointed to discover that there was no picture and only distorted sound from the ancient TV, so he snapped it off and sighed deeply. From what he had seen of the bedroom from the doorway, he had already decided he would sleep in the living room, but there didn't seem to be any heat other than the fireplace, and he didn't feel like starting a fire, so he stood up to find a blanket, when he heard it. Faintly from the backyard, a voice: a man's voice calling for help.

Damn, he thought. He'd been sloppy. It hadn't been a clean kill. He should have used a head shot, but he had just been so tired and hungry, and the man had gone down so easy. He'd have to finish the job fast before someone heard the man's cries for help. Grabbing the rifle, he headed out the back screen door.

The yard was empty. The charcoal still glowed in the grill, providing the only light besides that of the moon. He scanned the darkness. The old man's body was no longer on the ground where he had left him. *Where did he get to? Listen for the voice,* he told himself, *follow it and be quiet. He can't have gone far.*

A moan and a faint cry for help coming from the recesses of the Quonset hut. *So that's where he went. Well, he was trapped now. Like a wounded animal.* The boy walked steadily toward the open door, rifle leveled, already regretting with a glance up the street that he didn't visit the neighbors instead. Well, there was still time. He stepped into the darkened interior.

An old motorcycle blocked his path. He stepped around it and nearly ran into the carcass of a deer hanging from the rafters. Stacks of lumber and assorted pieces of junk lined the edges, while a tangled mess of ropes, fishing poles, tools and hunting bows hung from the walls.

The boy heard a cry of pain and stepped toward it. The old man was curled up in a corner under a tool bench. Holding the rifle steady, the boy saw the whites of the man's fearful eyes reflected in the moonlight.

"Please," the man pleaded in a shaky voice. The boy almost smiled as he raised and aimed the rifle for the easy kill. But then, just before pulling the trigger, he watched, almost in slow motion, as the man raised the bow with his trembling arms. Before the boy could react, he saw the old man let the string loose, heard a whoosh and felt a surge of shooting pain as the arrow struck deeply in his shoulder. The boy screamed before angrily firing a bullet into the man's head.

CHAPTER FORTY-EIGHT

Thank you so much for taking the time to speak to me, Pastor Carlsson. I know you were a very close friend to my Ethan. He's spoken so many times about his memories of summers at camp up on Bone Lake, but you have to promise me that you won't tell him that we spoke.

You know I met Ethan in college. I really wasn't there to learn anything, I was just looking for an "M.R.S." degree, I guess you'd have to say. And he was quite the catch. So strong and handsome and with a nice car to—all of my friends were so jealous. And always such a gentleman. My parents loved him.

So when he was recruited into the CIA and asked me to marry him, I could hardly say 'no' now, could I? A handsome man with a great career—he swept me off my feet. And for a while it was just like I dreamed it would be. Sure, we had to move all the time, and he always so busy, but I accepted my place and raised the children. But then...

I know I really shouldn't be unhappy. He has given me a wonderful life: two beautiful children. I got to travel–see the world, nice homes wherever we went. It's just...

I apologize for the tears. No, he has never mistreated me in that way. But...

It started in Singapore and got worse in Thailand. I knew he had needs—sexual needs—that I couldn't fulfill for him—men are like that you know, and that he had other women who he visited—local women. Frankly I didn't care... not much anyway. All the men did it—all the other wives agreed. So we played bridge and drank mai tais and ignored the bowling league—as we called the boy's nights out. Besides, we were tired at the end of the day raising kids and keeping house and it kept us from having to put up with their always grabbing, pushing and making a sticky mess all the time.

Don't get me wrong, I enjoy sex as much as the next girl, but the men are such cavemen when it comes to love making–always in a rush to get to where they want to go, that it is rarely much fun for their wives. The stupid fellows probably thought we were just clueless, but we all knew, and sex was something I was glad to "outsource" for the most part. I just had two rules: no diseases and I didn't want to hear about it. Everything was going along fine until...

I always knew he had a thing about Asian women. He didn't say anything, but he would always kind of stand at attention whenever he saw one of those cute little slant eyed sluts in their short, short schoolgirl skirt barely covering Mariana's trench. And they were oh so submissive. Not like us loudmouth American broads that speak our mind. He was attracted like a compass needle to a pole.

I didn't think much of it at the time, but I remember now hearing little things on the news reports. Of course it was all in that Asian gobbledygook – I never did learn anything except a few instructions for the maid, but it didn't strike me as odd at the time. But then when we were Bangkok, I kept seeing it happen more and I still didn't really put two and two together.

They said their bodies were mutilated—heads and hands cut off and other things: terrible thing. Those poor girls. They must have suffered horribly. They never caught who did it and I don't think they really cared very much because they were prostitutes and cheap bar girls.

I saw one of the girls' bodies when they pulled it out of a canal—I just happened along at the wrong time—and it looked so unreal, like one of my Barbie Dolls after my brother ripped the head off of it. So pale. Their skin that is–it isn't yellow you know, but more a translucent. The head was found a few feet away. They pulled it out by its long black hair. She couldn't have been more than 16.

Anyway, we were transferred back to D.C. right after that and I always wondered, was this perfect man—this wonderful loving father and husband... could he be capable of such violence? He's always been a hunter and all, even shot a lion on safari once, but...

So one night, after he retired, when he was out "bowling," I snuck into his closet in the basement and unlocked his steamer chest that he'd been lugging around for years and found… piles of photos, birthday cards, drawings the children made, paperwork, old clothes from college that no longer fit – just the usual memorabilia. I can tell you, I was so relieved and felt the love rush back into my heart to have my fears settled.

Only…

Something didn't seem right, so I took everything out and stacked it neatly. Ethan has never been sentimental. I didn't even know he had kept any of these things. When everything was removed, I could still hear things rattling around after it had been emptied, so I felt around and found a little release in the bottom corner. When I pulled the little handle, the bottom of the case lifted up.

There were seven of them, Pastor. I counted them, and then I closed the false bottom and placed everything back and have never said a word of this to anyone until now. Can you imagine how I feel when I look at him now? Seven pairs in all.

Yes, he kept their shoes—their strappy, sexy, red high heels. But even worse…

Their feet were still in them.

CHAPTER FORTY-NINE

In the months following Ken's death, Adele and Johnny broke off their wedding plans, and she and her family found themselves shunned by their neighbors. Adele's father was generally blamed by the community for allowing his red-haired girl into the mine and placing a curse over them all, and was given worse and lesser paying assignments at the mine. The other miners shunned him and even Johnny did not work with him if he could help it, and when they did work together, they worked in silence.

Adele watched sadly as her father's hair went gray quickly that summer, and he seemed even more tired than ever. He had packed his family across the ocean to find a better life and now he had lost his oldest son and found himself lucky that he even still had a job. An economic depression in 1893 had caused most of the mines in the region to close down, and the Mansfield—while still operating—suffered its share of unusual tribulations.

First, the pump on the sixth level of the Mansfield—a "wet" mine—whose drifts extended under the Michigamme River—was overworked and broke down, causing both the fifth and sixth levels to flood. Two more men fell down the timber shaft and died, and the men grumbled even more, while avoiding the Cornishman's unlucky presence. His continued employment was only due to the fact that he was among the best miners they had, and this was attributed to a rumored supernatural connection that the Cornish were said to have with the Tommyknockers—the mythical little men who lived in the mines and played tricks on miners they disliked, while helping those they did like to find the best veins.

Fall arrived and the prospects of a harsh winter ahead loomed like a black shroud over the family. Adele's father looked more pale and weary than ever—he was working even harder to try to make up for the loss of Ken's income. Adele pleaded with him in vain to rest; she constantly feared he would not last the winter at the rate he was wearing himself out. But he knew that his position was tenuous and that he needed to work as hard as he could while he still had the chance, with the hope that the other mines would reopen once the iron market recovered.

One September night Adele's father found himself assigned to the fifth level, down a damp and lonely drift. Before starting to work, he heard some creaking and noticed some shifting in the support timbers overhead and pointed it out to the supervisor when he came by.

"Eh, mind yer own, old man," the supervisor grumbled. "The planks will hold up. What's a matter, you afraid of a little water dripping on ya? Just do your job."

Adele's father swallowed his concern, and turned back to work chipping away at the cave wall with a sigh. He soon found his familiar rhythm and filled the ore car with the debris containing the iron ore that he knocked out of the side of the wall. The boys pushed the car down the tracks to the skip, dumped the contents into the bucket and rang the bell to notify the skip tender to raise the ore to the surface where it would be carted away and separated.

The older man took off his soft cap, sat down and rested for a moment in the candlelight and listened to the sound of the river rushing overhead. It was always a disconcerting sound —he had never really gotten used to the it—but it seemed different tonight— maybe louder?

Suddenly the creaking in the support beams intensified. His body tensed as he listened carefully for changes in the usual sounds he was accustomed to hearing in the mine. Suddenly, there was a rumble overhead that grew louder and erupted into a huge crash as the roof of the Number One shaft caved in and the full weight of the river rushed into the mine. The ground shook violently and Adele's father heard the shouts of men echoing above a furious torrent of water. The three blasts of the whistle sounded into the night and he rushed quickly toward the main shaft.

Once there, he saw a waterfall cascading down from the levels above. He watched as the skip rose then lowered through the gushing deluge to the fourth level, where the night boss jumped out and ran into the drift, shouting warnings to his men.

On the side wall, men attempted to climb to safety fighting the heavy streams of water crashing all around them. A rush of water pushed a man off the ladder and he fell screaming past him as Adele's father reached for the ladder rung.

Then he remembered something and hesitated for a moment before he turned and struggled back into the drift—fighting against the swelling tide rushing down the tunnel and into the shaft.

Turning down one side tunnel, he dodged to one side as a man was swept past him and was carried down and over the edge.

"Johnny!" Adele's father called—his voice barely audible over the thundering cacophony of the powerful onrush. He did not hear a response and considered retreating back to the main shaft while he could, when...

"Here," he suddenly heard the young man's voice calling from within a chamber. He struggled into the cavern against the powerful undulating force, he saw the young Finn barely clinging to a rock and frozen in fear.

190

He grabbed the young man and—propelled headlong by the rushing waves, hurried him out of the cave—half running, half sliding—down the drift to the main shaft, where they just managed to grab onto the wall in time to avoid being swept over the brink. Pushing Johnny onto the ladder, Adele's father had just enough to time to yell, "Climb!" before the ceiling in the level collapsed completely and a thunderous mass of waves engulfed him.

After the disaster, the company—who was found responsible for the disaster by the authorities — originally told the families of the 27 men that they could stay in their homes as long as they wanted, and that they would receive compensation for their loss; but after two months the widows and children received their eviction notices. On moving day, while packing up their household, Adele noticed a man nervously standing in the bushes watching the house. After some time, Johnny approached the house, cap in hand and asked for Adele.

"I heard you were leaving and thought you could use another hand packing up."

"I suppose it would be useful to have another man to help," Adele's mother interjected as she walked by carrying a box. Her brothers greeted Johnny warily—they had not seen him since their father's funeral, as they continued loading the family's belongings into a wagon that waited outside.

"Where are you going?" Johnny asked the girl.

"Crystal Falls," Adele replied blankly. "My mother's cousin has a boardinghouse and we are going to help her with it."

"Adele, I…"

"Don't say anything. This is hard enough as it is."

"Your father… he saved my life."

The girl stayed silent. Johnny found his voice.

"I wish you wouldn't."

"Wouldn't what?"

"Go."

"Why do you care. Don't you know I am the curse? Me and my stupid red hair killed my father and all those men."

"Don't be silly. That is just a superstition."

"If it is, then why has everyone avoided me since the accident? I have been treated as though I have the plague. And you…Why did you abandon me?"

"I was… stupid. But I know better now. I feel like I've grown ten years these last few months. I know what I want now."

"And what is that?" she whispered.

"You," he said simply. "The mine has hired me on to clean up the mess and get the mine back up and running. They say it should take over a year and then I can go back to mining. They've allowed me to rent a house. Your house in fact."

"Oh Johnny," she sobbed.

"It is a living," he continued. "Adele, I want you. And if you stay with me, we could make a new start. I know the mine may kill me in the end, but at least we have a chance. Do you really want to live at a boardinghouse? Or will you stay… and live with me?"

"But the wedding…"

"I talked to your preacher and we can say our vows now in your church, and your family, they can be with us to celebrate before they leave. I know it is not what we planned, but—"

"Yes," she said and kissed him.

The wedding was an unqualified success. Adele's brothers and sisters celebrated until evening fell and then they headed out of town. Johnny's family attended reluctantly at first, but grew into the spirit and welcomed the red-haired woman fully into their hearts and family. Adele never saw her mother again, as she died shortly after she arrived in Crystal Falls. The remaining family waited for years for the compensation promised to them by the company that never did arrive.

CHAPTER FIFTY

"You know what we have to do," Jeremy snarled.

He and Junior stood in front of the locked room in the basement.

"No, we can't...." Junior said dumbly.

"We have to."

"She said to never—"

"We have to, Junior. You know we do. Once inside, maybe we'll find a clue to where she is."

"I can't do it," Junior. "She said she would—"

"What did she say she would do if you opened this door?"

"—leave me..."

"Well, she's done that already, hasn't she? That is if you are telling the truth about not having anything to do with her gone missing—which I still don't believe. But if you are telling the truth for once in your life, then she's gone and left you, and you are too much of a pussy to break down this door to find out where she went."

"Shut the fuck up. She's coming back. I know she is. She's probably just over in Fargo with her cousin hiding out and making me pay for something I did or didn't do. But when she comes home and sees that I broke my promise..."

"She'll what?"

"She'll leave for good. She made me promise. It's her room."

"I know it's her damn room. She never let me in when I was a kid either. Said she was afraid I'd break her fucking dolls."

"It was her room. It is her room, dammit. She said that was the one thing that she had to have when she first agreed to stay with me."

"So what's in there besides some stupid dolls?"

"I don't know. She used to go in there and lock the door when she got sad."

"I know. I remember. Why was she so sad all the time?"

"How the hell should I know. She's a woman. Oh hell, it was probably about your dad. I think she kept pictures of him in there. She'd sit in there and burn incense—used to smell that shit all the time and I'm allergic to it— she didn't care — and do whatever: cry, pout —drugs I suppose, although I tried to keep them away from her."

"Bullshit, you were her source."

"Yeah, well be glad I was. If it wasn't me, she would have got ahold of them somewhere. At least I made sure she got the best quality and I kept her on a strict regiment."

"You gave her just enough to keep her hooked," Jeremy growled and clenched his fist. "So she wouldn't leave you."

"Maybe so, but I hate to tell you this, punk, but your sweet momma is a full-fledged drug addict."

"You could've got her help or something—"

"Yeah right. In case you didn't notice, your mother doesn't take direction well."

"Well, whatever. I am busting down this door."

"Kid, I wouldn't. I'm telling you. I tried forcing my way in one time and she gave me a look like I'll never forget—like she'd poison me in my sleep if I forced the issue. She said she'd do anything for me, but she had to have this one thing—a place to go… a place just for herself"

Jeremy sniffed. "Did you notice there is kind of a rotten smell coming from in there?"

"My nose ain't what it once was, Jeremy. Please don't tell me you smell anything. Please don't say that."

"You don't think—?"

"We got some folks say they saw her driving north out of town—what do you think she abandoned her car and came home and went in there alone and…?"

"Give me that flashlight." Jeremy got down on his hands and knees and stared under the door. "I don't see anything…"

"I couldn't take that. I just couldn't take that," Junior stammered sinking to his knees.

"Don't suppose you have a spare key anywhere?" Jeremy asked standing up.

"No…"

"You're a cop. You can open any lock."

"No, I won't—'

"You are awfully nervous about opening this door, Junior. Like maybe you've got more reasons than just being afraid of my mom?"

"I ain't afraid of her, and I told you before I would never hurt her."

"Then we're going to have to… take this door down."

"No Jeremy, I can't. You can't do that. She'll blame me. Something will happen. You'll knock over a shelf and break her dolls."

"Fuck the dolls."

Jeremy dug through some tools and grabbed a sledgehammer and taking a big swing, struck a massive blow at the door.

"No." Junior covered his eyes.

The door took several more blows before it splintered enough for Jeremy to reach a hand through and unlock it.

"Be careful damn you!" shouted Junior.

Jeremy flipped the wall switch and a single bare bulb hanging from the ceiling illuminated the interior. In the center of the room was a card table covered by a patterned tablecloth, with a folding chair placed behind it. The table was covered with some half-finished attempts at needlework, an incense burner, a large teacup, some gossip magazines and a Bible, and an ashtray filled with ashes and a well-used crack pipe. Jeremy took a step into the room and kicked a half full garbage can which released a cloud of foul fumes directly to his nostrils. He bent over and examine the contents, several beer bottles, the mushy remains of an apple core, a molding banana peel and a bag of what appeared to be rotten broccoli and carrots.

"Here's your smell, Junior."

"Oh thank God, thank God. She's not there, right? We can fix this door. Replace it and she might not know." Junior ran into the other room to look for some wood and tools to patch the door.

Jeremy scanned the room—buckets, rags and coffee cans on the floor—blankets, clothes, fabric and yarn piled on shelves. On one shelf he spotted some photo albums. He opened one and saw a picture of his mother as a young woman standing in a backyard with a tall dark-haired young man, of approximately the same age — possibly Preacher? next to her, while a shorter blond young man who he knew was his father grinned and held a screaming baby he recognized as himself in his arms. He closed the book quickly as though he had opened someone's diary by mistake and slid it to one side with the intent of examining it later.

The other shelves held a radio, some photos of his father and himself in frames, a paperback copy of Balzac's "Lost Illusions," some childish and inexpensive knickknacks, some jewelry boxes filled with cheap costume jewelry, several copies of "The Watchtower," several open boxes crammed with spools of thread, playing cards and baby toys, and a hand drawn Valentine card with the words '*Hey Darlin!*' scrawled across a heart.

Jeremy sighed. No note, no map, nothing to indicate where his mother could be.

"So Junior, where are these precious dolls anyway?"

Junior's muffled reply was inaudible from the other room.

Just then Jeremy spotted them—a row of seven shoeboxes arranged neatly across the top row of the shelving unit. They were laid atop a piece of gold and purple velvet fabric, while several candles had been placed in arrangement around them as though the boxes were being displayed on an altarpiece.

Jeremy noticed the step stool and hesitated. He remembered his mother's moods and how he used to hear her crying and wondered what she was doing in this room for hours at a time. He knew that he was now entering into dangerous territory—prying into his mother's darkest and most private secrets, and he shuddered to think that he could find things he was not ever supposed to know about, nor would want to discover.

He stepped up on the step and with trembling hands picked up the first box. It was lighter than he thought it would be, as though it were merely filled with scraps of paper, or possibly sawdust, or even the hollow bones of birds. Jeremy climbed down, sat on the chair and placed the box carefully on the table.

He stared at the box for what seemed an eternity. Finally, with an immense feeling of dread tightening the knot in his stomach, he reached out and slowly removed the lid.

A musty perfumed smell exhaled from the opened box. Nestled within the interior was what appeared to be a small child with its eyes closed. Jeremy reached in and carefully removed the small, fragile body gently, fearing that with the slightest pressure it would crumble into dust.

The girl was dressed in a handmade dress of calico and lace. The flesh tone-colored paint on the weathered porcelain face was chipped on one half of the sleeping face, while spidery cracks covered the other side like black veins.

Jeremy carefully held the delicate doll up to the light. The air within the cramped room was stale and heavy, and within the closed-in surroundings, he felt dizzy and as if he could hardly breathe.

As he tilted her, the doll suddenly opened her eyes.

"Mama," she said in a high-pitched, mechanical croak.

CHAPTER FIFTY-ONE

So how did you track me down? I'm not Betty Jensen anymore you know. Changed my name to Tiffany Nightcloud a few years ago when I started dancing. Yeah, I know I'm no spring chicken, but you'd be surprised what money guys will pay to see a woman, any woman, naked, and I've managed to keep myself in decent shape. Yes, I know I got bags under the eyes and plenty of wrinkles, but they ain't looking at my face anyway.

I do a bit of entertaining on the side, as you may have expected. A girl's gotta live you know. And if you're interested later… I know the face ain't too pretty, but you can always put a flag over her face and fuck her for Ol' Glory, like the GIs round here like to say. Well think it over, anyway. I'll give you a deal.

Truly, I don't know how the hell you found me in Houston. I told everybody I was going to Florida after I sold the place. Ended up hooking up with this crazy Indian guy named Lightcloud—I changed my name later to Nightcloud because it sounds better for this business—me working nights and all—but anyway we somehow blew through all the money I made from the bar in less than a year. Don't remember much about that time, but I know we were in Vegas for a bit and then Frsico and maybe Miami, and there was a bunch of coke involved.

Yeah I knew the kid that killed my husband, and yes I was there when it happened—and you know what? I do feel a little sorry he got sent up river, because that Chester was one mean sonofabitch and it served him right. But at least Jeremy only got stuck in Juvie and got out when he turned 18, so it wasn't so bad.

Buy me another drink and I'll tell you the whole story. They don't put any booze in the girls' drinks 'cuz they don't want us falling down drunk onstage, but I always keep a little bottle or two hidden away and spike the crap they give us. Had a few already tonight and I'm actually feeling pretty buzzed. That's a good boy.

So yeah, that day fucking Ches is out there a hollerin' and then he throws a perfectly good 12-pack against the wall, like the imbecile he always was, and is going on ranting and raving about how he's gonna beat me up again. He'd already hit one of the boys and he was kicking the shit out of poor Jeremy, and I thought, oh fuck, I'm next and I decided I better get the baseball bat I keep behind the bar just in case. But then Jeremy, God love him, he jumps up out of the blue and smacks Ches right square in the head. Just about the funniest thing I ever saw.

Two of the other boys that ran away came back real quick and were all shook up, what with all the blood and Jesse— I mean Jeremy killin' the bastard, and they was weeping and wailing and making a scene. But I just said "there, there" all motherly-like, and had them carry the poor kid into the bar.

He looked a bloody mess, but he was breathing and I'd seen enough bar fights to know he'd be just fine once he got his wits back. So I gave the other boys each a soda, called my buddy Junior, the Sheriff, and told him what happened, and he couldn't believe it and was swearing up a storm, and he said he'd be right over. Then I told the boys to calm down and I went back out check on Ches, just to make sure, and he started to roll over and had that stupid grin on his face and was asking what happened, so… I gave him a couple quick taps on the noggin with the bat and that was that. No harm done, he was reported dead already.

Was pretty sure they wouldn't send the kid to big boy prison and so I swore up and down that it was Jeremy what done it, but in self-defense, which it was. Was pretty sick of the bar business anyway and I knew a couple people looking to buy it. Worked out great for everyone, except maybe Ches. Ha!

Now you don't tell anyone, you promise? We gotta respect the statue of limitations now don't we, because she's blind and a woman and only women bleed, if you know what I mean. That's all just water under the Paint River Bridge now and there's no need to go raising a stink over spilled milk or blood now, right?

I'll bet it was my sister that told you where I was, wasn't it? She's the only one that knows, except for Bobby down in Dallas. It wasn't Bobby was it?

Yeah, yeah fuck you too, Leon, I hear you. I'll be there in a minute. Yeah, right. Kiss it! Well, it's time for me to go back on.

But you—you don't go leaving now. You just stick around and we can talk some more after I do my routine. You'll like it, I'm pretty limber for a gal my age. Besides, I like talking to you, you're funny. You're sweet. Stick around and buy me another drink and I'll give you a private lap dance later that you'll never forget.

CHAPTER FIFTY-TWO

Jeremy and Junior stood facing each other in the clearing with their pistols drawn.

"What are you doing following me?" Junior growled. "And where'd you get that piece?"

"I'm following you because you are a real piece of shit, and the gun's my girlfriend's. I borrowed it."

"Girlfriend? You just got back in town."

"What can I say, I'm resourceful."

"But that still doesn't answer my first question—why the fuck are you following me?"

"Why didn't you tell me they found my father's body?"

"I just found out myself, and they don't know it's him for sure yet."

"So are you getting nervous yet, Junior? They gonna find out you were the one who killed him?"

"What? Oh hell no, I had nothing to do with it."

"Who did?"

"I don't know, but I have a pretty good idea."

"Who is it?'

"Drop your gun and I might consider telling you someday."

"I ain't dropping nothing until you tell me what you are doing out here at Bone Lake."

"I'm looking for your Mom."

"Looking for her? Why here, why now?"

"If you must know, Fred Arnold was at the debate. He gave me call a bit ago. He didn't even know Jenny was missing until now. His cabin is just down the road and he said he thought he saw her driving up here a few days ago. Said he's seen her up here before."

"Bullshit. I don't believe you. Where is she Junior? What have you done to her, you bastard? This whole story about somebody maybe seeing her car is just another bunch of your crap. You probably set all this up just to get me out in the middle of nowhere. So what are you going to do now, kill me and blame what you did to my mom on me? Think that insane story will fly with the people in town?"

"I oughta' shoot you down like the no good punk loser you are," Junior snarled, "but you got it dead wrong. How many times do I gotta tell you I didn't kill her! I love your mom. Why do you think I put up with your shit all these years?"

"I don't believe you, Junior. I don't believe you about my dad and I don't believe you about my mom. She knew I was getting out and wouldn't have just run off without a word. I only came back to this lame ass town for her. Otherwise I'd be in Florida or California or someplace way the fuck away from here."

"Just shut your smart mouth up and go home Jeremy—you're in over your head."

"Why don't you make me, old man!"

"Yeah, you're a tough one with a gun in your hand. Why don't you try it without the piece? I always could whip your ass."

"You outweighed me by a ton back then and I was just a kid. You ain't ever whipping me again."

Both men threw their guns to the ground and, launching their bodies together, began pummeling each other with their fists. Junior still had a huge weight advantage and was surprisingly quick, but Jeremy's wiry body was faster, and the younger man got in some quick hits, catching Junior with a quick left to the face, causing a stream of blood to pour from his nose. In response, the sheriff roared in anger and slammed Jeremy against a tree with a thud. They fell, tumbling through brush, down an embankment and slid down the damp earth into a mud hole, where, enraged, they wallowed around—splashing in the sloppy mess, slipping and falling as they tried unsuccessfully to gain an advantage over each other.

Frustrated, and finding himself out of breath, Jeremy suddenly looked up and realized with a shock that they were being watched. A boy stood above on the ridge, his rifle pointed at the two men.

"Whoa, hold on there, son," Junior stammered and scrambled quickly out of the mud like a sea lion flopping onto dry land. Jeremy stared at the boy and slowly stood up, his entire covered with dripping muck.

The boy stood silent and sad for a minute, then he sighed deeply and lowered his gun. He gestured for the men to follow as he turned and walked into the trees. Jeremy and Junior scrambled up the slope and followed after the boy.

"Hold on there. Where are you going?" Junior huffed out of breath.

The exhausted boy did not speak, but just raised his arm— revealing the broken shaft of an arrow embedded in his blood-soaked shoulder—and pointed at a deep, brush-covered ravine just off the road.

"There," the boy said in a quiet voice.

The two men rushed to the spot. Peering into the heavy foliage, they could just make out a dark shape within the shadows of the thicket. Moving closer—fighting their way through a barrier of tall wild grass and overgrown vegetation, the shape became clearer to them, until it was finally revealed to be that of a car: a car wedged into the ditch at an abrupt angle and completely hidden from view by the trees and thick underbrush surrounding it on all sides.

"Shit!" Junior exhaled.

Jeremy was already at the car door. Tearing it open, he found his mother's battered and bloody body hanging limply from her shoulder belt.

"Oh Christ, Jenny!" Junior moaned. "Is she?"

Tears trickled down his face, as Jeremy gently pulled his mother's cold and lifeless body from the car, whispering, "Mom, I'm here!" in her ear as he did.

They lay her down in the grass and sunlight and she suddenly stirred slightly and coughed weakly. Her eyes opened but did not focus. Her mouth moved, but could form no words.

"She's still breathing," Jeremy cried in joy.

"Get her to the car, fast!" Junior snapped.

"What are you doing?"

"I'll grab our guns and meet you at the hospital."

"Where's the kid?" They looked up to see there was only empty space where the kid once stood.

"He's gone. Hurry up, I'll be right there." Junior pushed Jeremy away. and disappeared into the trees.

Jeremy picked up and carried his mother, who shivered, moaned slightly and fell back into unconsciousness. Her broken leg dangled loosely, as her son lugged her up the ravine and quickly back down the road to his car. He carefully laid her in the back seat and lifted a water bottle to her lips. She awoke with a gasp and drank greedily.

"Don't worry Mom," Jeremy spoke softly as he stroked his mother's cheek. I'll get you to the hospital. You're going to be alright. I was so scared that you left me. I thought maybe he'd hurt you. I'll never leave you again. I'll never let him hurt you."

Climbing quickly into the driver's seat, he started his car and pulled away, just as a single gunshot echoed from the woods.

CHAPTER FIFTY-THREE

Adele awoke just past midnight to whistle blasts, frightened voices shouting and horses neighing in panic. Wrapping a heavy blanket around her baby, she carried him close to her as she made her way frantically out the door of the shack—her heart pounding—her fears focused on her Johnny, ensconced deep in the gloomy depths of the mine.

Stopping and standing still—surveying the scene surrounding her—she stared in stunned shock and dismay as a familiar red glow illuminating the horizon in the distance grew in intensity as it swiftly advanced upon the town.

"Wildfire? No, not again?" she whispered, as holding the whimpering infant tightly, and—despairing for their safety, and that of the world itself, she turned her teary eyes to the stars and shouted curses toward God in her mind.

CHAPTER FIFTY-FOUR

I could hear him breathing in the darkness of my room.

Withdraw thine hand far from me: and let not thy dread make me afraid.

"So, you've come?" I asked the shadow quietly.

"Yes," he replied in a low voice.

"You know… everything?"

"Yes, my stepfather told me."

"He doesn't know it all."

"He knows enough."

"Yes, I suppose he does… I saw he won his reelection."

"Uh huh." The dark shape moved quietly across the room toward me. *If I screamed would anyone hear?* I wondered.

"So what happened to the CIA guy?"

"He's gone. Left town in humiliation. Got a lot of shit for beating up an old man at the debate who was only defending his wife's honor. Funny thing is his wife stayed here. She's working for Pastor Carlsson now."

"Catching that kid who kidnapped Jenny and then killing him must have sealed the deal. He's a real hero to the townsfolk now, I guess."

"Yeah, right 'kidnapped.' Oh, he's a hero alright," the voice answered scornfully.

"How is your mother?"

"She's tough. She's been through a lot, but she is going to make it."

"Yes, she always does."

He stood silently in the shadows by the side of the bed as the seconds became eons.

"Well, if you are going to do it..." I finally broke the silence.

"Yeah. Sorry Preacher."

"I know, Jeremy."

"But you did kill my father and little sister."

"That I did..."

Are not my days few? cease then, and let me alone, that I may take comfort a little,

I see again the things from my life: Jenny's face aglow as she teased me by the water's edge; the three of us laughing after robbing the drug store; Jesse and I in the canoe on the Paint River...

How can I leave them—my memories? Should I scream? But no—it is all dust now. Let it go.

"An eye for an eye. That's what the Bible says, right?"

"Yes. And now you and Junior can run this town."

"We've got some plans."

Whoso rewardeth evil for good, evil shall not depart from his house.

"Can't have any loose ends."

"No we can't." he said and leaned in closer.

Before I go whence I shall not return, even to the land of darkness and the shadow of death; A land of darkness, as darkness itself; and of the shadow of death, without any order, and where the light is as darkness.

"But son..."

"What?"

209

Which rejoice exceedingly, and are glad, when they can find the grave?

I looked into the eyes of the man in the dark and saw the face of the young boy I once held in my arms—looking so much like his father Jesse—my eidolon, now turned into my angel of deliverance.

Rejoice, O young man, in thy youth; and let thy heart cheer thee in the days of thy youth, and walk in the ways of thine heart, and in the sight of thine eyes: but know thou, that for all these things God will bring thee into judgment.

Therefore remove sorrow from thy heart, and put away evil from thy flesh: for childhood and youth are vanity.

"Watch your back, Jeremy. And promise me you'll take care of your mom for me. I loved her once."

"I will, Preacher, I promise."

"Do it now then. I am ready. And Jeremy… thank you."

He took the pillow in his hands and pressed it firmly against my face as I struggled to breath. Despite my desire, fear took hold of my heart and my mind refused to gently accept its fate.

All things come alike to all: there is one event to the righteous, and to the wicked; to the good and to the clean, and to the unclean; to him that sacrificeth, and to him that sacrificeth not: as is the good, so is the sinner…

I knew the end was coming and could feel my burden lifting as let go and was glad of it.

For the living know that they shall die: but the dead know not any thing, neither have they any more a reward; for the memory of them is forgotten.

Pain, terror, then at last… ecstasy, when I was finally released from my broken shell out of this hellish world and into darkness with the distant hope of light.

CHAPTER FIFTY-FIVE

He came in late and slid into bed next to her. She felt the perspiration on his arms as he huddled next to her and held her tight.

"Mmmm I'm glad you're here," she whispered sleepily. "What took you so long?"

"Sorry I'm so late, but I had some things to finish up."

"All done now?"

"I think so."

"Everything OK?"

"Just tired I guess. Sooo tired…"

"Well get some sleep."

"I'll have to start looking for a job tomorrow."

"You're going to stay?" she asked, brightening.

"Where else would I go?"

She smiled in the dark, her eyes closed to keep in the tears.

They lay silently for several minutes before Jeremy broke the silence.

"Hey one thing that's been bugging me," he whispered thoughtfully. "Who's the lady in photo hanging on the wall over there."

"Oh, that's my great-granny Adele."

"She looks like you."

"Everbody says that."

Jeremy studied the red-haired woman in the photo.

"So what's her story?"

"Oh she was a pretty neat old lady. I don't remember much about her. Guess she had a pretty rough life—her dad died when the mine flooded. She married my Great Grandpa John and they lived here in Crystal Falls after Mansfield burned down the second time. He worked for some of the mines around here I think. She had my Grandma and her brothers and sisters and then she… died."

"Same old story."

"Yup, same old story."

Jeremy pressed his body against Katy's back and felt a sense of relief as her warm living nature entered him—momentarily taking away the chill of death and pulling him deeper into the dark and pleasant sleep of the satisfied.

CHAPTER FIFTY-SIX

They say I will make a full recovery. The doctors are amazed at my rapid return to health and the people of the town have gone out of their way to comfort me with tender care and exuberant displays of well wishing—embracing the wayward girl into their arms like never before—treating me as a symbol of our town's fortitude and will to overcome against all odds.

My husband has been re-elected, in no small part to my tale of captivity and rescue. Junior has coached me well in what to say and what not to. I tell them all that I do not remember much of my ordeal, only that deranged boy and his gun holding me against my will in a remote cabin. That terrible sad and lonely boy who heard my cry.

That boy, who without his help, I would no doubt have perished alone, in a ravine in my car just off the road to Bone Lake. That boy Tim, who is dead now, another sacrifice to the continuation of the lie that is my life. How I wish no one had found me and I had died when I took that wrong turn and slid down the embankment and into the thick underbrush alone and unseen. But, I seem to have a way of enduring car crashes, not unlike that one so many years ago with my dear Preacher, rest his soul, when I first learned the meaning of sacrifice.

Junior believes I was running away from him. He should know better—I am too big a coward to leave, but let him suffer as I have suffered so many times over the years from his evil seed. Let him cower at my wrath always, and let him wonder, always wonder what was in my mind. But he will never really know what I was doing, because I will never tell him.

For you see my path to Bone Lake was one I have taken many times throughout the years. Sometimes in pain; sometimes in anger, but always wracked with guilt and with the weight of my sins dragging me deeper and drowning me in the cold, dark waters of eternal sadness. I intend on returning, once I have regained my health and resumed walking and driving, whenever Junior is away and unaware. I will not linger long, but will always be sure to cut fresh wildflowers and lay them with care upon the ground under the big trees on the rise overlooking the lake and on the seven secret graves of my unnamed babies.

ABOUT THE AUTHOR

Brad Walseth is an American novelist, screenwriter, musician and photographer currently living near Chicago. Born and raised in the mountainous region of Western Montana, Brad worked in a lumber mill, played in rock bands and hitchhiked around the West. before graduating from the University of Montana with a B.A. in English Literature. Brad worked for several years in radio and television before relocating to Chicago, where he attended Northwestern University and worked as a stockbroker, a postal clerk and as a corporate communications writer. During these years, Brad's short stories and reviews began appearing in publications nationwide, while his several years of rock journalism on the groundbreaking music website Concertlivewire.com led to his starting JazzChicago.net, where he juggled responsibilities as publisher, editor-in-chief, photographer, primary writer and interviewer. Brad was co-host and producer of the popular radio show, "Jazz, Chicago Style," while also working as an award-winning magazine writer/editor. One of Brad's screenplays, a "mockumentary" about a garage band who burn down their garage and have to become a carport band ("Hug the Shrugs"), was made into a independent film in 2004. Brad first novel ("The Courier") was recently translated into Spanish. "Crystal Falls"— a literary crime novel, was originally published by Satalyte Publishing in 2014.

Made in the USA
Columbia, SC
25 September 2020